# An Unexpected Beginning

## By Mary Starner

# *Copyright*

First Edition: February 2015

# *Table of Contents*

# *Dedication*

## *Dedicated to Room 18, Hillview School's Class of 1972-73*

# *Journey*

**★★★★**

Rainy days have a way of making even the best student antsy. Today was no exception, rather it was worse. Along with the rain there was the forceful, howling wind that kept slamming the windows and driving torrents of rain against the walls so that the classrooms seemed caught in the middle of a hurricane.

At lunch time, Mr. Reynolds showed a film in an effort to keep the students entertained but the young ones soon became restless and this was as catching as chickenpox. All the teachers eating lunch groaned at the riot of noise as the children burst out of the multipurpose room to return to their classes. They all agreed that the afternoon ahead with that loud bunch of wild indians might be a nightmare. "Well at least we can send them home in a few hours," thought Mrs. Stern, "I'm glad they aren't mine for twenty-four hours a day!"

Back in room eighteen, twenty-eight fourth graders were finally settled in their seats to take their Friday spelling test after the flurry of excitement caused by the class mascot, a cat named Rascal. That wet feline cried at the door to be let in but surprised everyone by bringing with him a bedraggled, dripping, little half-grown, calico kitten. Kristi and Beth were allowed to wipe the cats down with paper towels and settle them on the rug in the reading corner before the test began.

As she gave the dictation sentences Martha Stern noticed the sky growing darker rapidly; the wind increasing in violence. She was thankful that concentrating on the spelling was keeping her students from noticing. Suddenly that concentration was broken by the violent shaking of the building and a deafening roar. The windows clamped shut with a sticky thud.

"Earthquake!" Mike shouted.

"Nonsense, I think it's just the storm," replied Mrs. Stern, "but to be on the safe side in case a window breaks everybody duck and cover."

Secretly Mrs. Stern wondered if the building could withstand the wind without collapsing. She'd never seen wind like this. At least the desks would offer some protection. The movement of the building was so violent some of the children might even get seasick she worried. Then the lights went out followed by the loudest crack anyone had ever heard!

Just as suddenly the following silence seemed deafening. The room felt suspended but moving, not shaking. Vicki and Amy were sobbing with fright. The ever gabby Tom was speechless.

"I can't see anything outside," whined Mike who sat closest to the windows.

"Open the door and look out," suggested Russ.

"No! Don't do that," snapped Mrs. Stern who had the vague feeling that it would be very wrong to try the door. "Everyone sit in their seats and we'll finish the spelling test."

"But Mrs. Stern, it's really too dark to see the paper enough to write," protested Barry.

"I guess you're right," agreed Mrs. Stern. Boys and girls I feel we must act very carefully, and think before we do anything, because something very strange is happening." Twenty-eight pairs of frightened eyes turned to stare at their teacher.

************

Mr. Reynolds leaned against the wall in his office and tried to get to the bell button to sound the duck and cover drill, but before he could manage this seemingly simple task in his quaking office, the lights went out signaling a loss of power.

Mrs. Holly, the school secretary called. "What should we do? It's almost like a Midwest tornado."

"Just wait it out and hope the staff can keep the pupils from panic. I hope the building holds up. You'd better get under your desk," Mr. Reynolds yelled.

Then came the loudest crack they'd ever heard and both suspected the worst, as did Mrs. Thomas in her house across the street. "I hope my son is O.K." she prayed.

Just as suddenly as it rose the wind died down and the rain let up. Mr. Reynolds and Mrs. Holly, joined by an anxious Mrs. Thomas, went hurrying down the corridor to see what had caused that awesome crack. They were relieved to find nothing but a few broken windows in the first two wings.

Suddenly their worst fears were realized. Where room eighteen had been there was nothing but a gaping hole. One wall of Mrs. Gunther's classroom was missing and the terrified fifth graders were huddled with their teacher against the opposite wall. What was left of the room was a jumbled mess.

"I'm here, oh help me please!" moaned Chris from the top of the baseball backstop. His broken leg was bent at an odd angle.

"We're all here except Steve", a trembling Mrs. Gunther volunteered. "And Chris is over there."

"They're gone! Oh they're all gone off in the sky just like Dorothy in The Wizard of Oz.," wept Mrs. Hall as she ran across the athletic field toward the gathering crowd. "I was looking out of my kitchen window and I saw the end of the building rip off and sail away just like a cardboard box. The two boys in the room next door were at the chalkboard; one of them fell off and landed on the backstop. The other one was trying to hang on."

Everyone looked as she pointed and following that direction

they all saw that Steve had not been able to hang on long. His crumpled body lay draped in the notch formed by the sawn off tops of a recently pruned eucalyptus tree across the street. The silence of the puzzled, frightened people was finally broken by Mr. Reynolds who murmured something about calling an ambulance for Chris and notifying the superintendent as he hurried toward the office. The custodian and the vice principal held back the stunned crowd of students staring at the empty space occupied just a short time earlier by a building housing a classroom full of children. Twenty-eight children and one adult had vanished completely.

# *Strange Journey*

### ✱✱✱✱

"I don't think we should open the doors until we can see what's going on, or someone comes to our rescue," advised Mrs. Stern. "We seem to be moving and if that is true then we might fall out!"

"But Mrs. Stern, if that's true it's mighty strange, especially without damage," reasoned Barry.

"I know, that's why I feel this is strange. We can't see out the windows and we seem to be traveling at a great rate yet the building has not collapsed and we are able to breathe. With everything shut so tight you'd think we would have exhausted the oxygen in here by now. But we haven't. So boys and girls let's just wait and see what happens next. It appears we'll be here a long time so we have to make plans."

"Does anyone have any food left at all from their lunch?" questioned the teacher. A few hands went up. "By the way, I think until we land someplace we had better move carefully. Think of this room as a boat you wouldn't want to tip over so we don't all rush from place to place or gather in one spot at the same time. Now Jenny, what do you have?"

"Well I have two cases of Girl Scout cookies I was to deliver this afternoon."

"How lucky for us. Jeremy?"

"I saved my apple to eat after school."

"Good! Did anyone else save fruit to eat later? Marvelous!"

The short list on the board added up to three apples, two oranges, one box of forbidden Sweet Tarts and the cookies. Not much to hold off starvation.

"Now did you all remember coats or sweaters this morning? Please, one at a time collect yours and hang it on the back of your chair so we can see who doesn't have one. Then if there is something left in the lost and found box we can use it," instructed their teacher.

Soon all the chairs had at least a sweater or a coat, sometimes two, draped over the back. Annette had quite a collection. Being rather forgetful at times, she always ended up with more at school than she took home in the afternoon.

"Now your coat or sweater will have to be used as a cover for sleeping. We can settle several people on the rug with the pillows. Others will use the floor and hats, gloves, or whatever we can find to use as pillows. If this mysterious journey lasts more than one night we'll take turns on the rug. We'll conserve all we can so no drawing or sharpening of pencils until it is absolutely necessary."

"Since it appears to be after school by my watch you may play games quietly or finish your weaving, read or do what you want. Within reason of course. At six o'clock we'll divide the fruit and have one cookie each."

"What about Rascal and Raquel?" Betsy asked.

"Oh heavens, I forgot about them," she groaned. "I do have an envelope of kitty crumbles left from the treat I bring for Rascal, so I'll ration them as long as I can," Mrs. Stern replied.

It was a sad group that finally settled into an uncomfortable, exhausted sleep; all of them wondering what was going to happen and missing their families so.

Mrs. Stern napped fitfully, wrapped in her coat with her head on her desk. What a responsibility! She'd never expected to be in charge of a class permanently. Oh how she missed her own family. What would happen to them?

Sometime near three a.m. by her watch she woke again and stood up to stretch. Looking out into the black void beyond the windows, her eyes straining for anything remotely familiar, she spied something that confirmed all her fears. Becoming aware of another sleepless person she beckoned Ron to join her at the window.

"Is that what I think it is?" she whispered, pointing to a distant, glimmering ball to their right almost out of range of normal sight.

"If you mean earth, that's what I think too," he replied softly.

Quickly, quietly, she woke Barry, Stacy, Ricky and Gary and asked them to observe also, so there would be no doubt that what she and Ron had seen was not just an illusion.

"Be very quiet and don't wake the others. We don't need panic and they need sleep," she cautioned.

In silent desperation they watched the last glimpse of their home planet disappear swiftly from sight. Then each returned to lay sleepless and wondering, until sleep finally overcame them once again.

How was it possible for anything so flimsily constructed to withstand the pressures of such swift space flight? How could it move without an energy source? How were they able to breathe in the airless void of space? Why was this happening to them?

Finally that last heart-rending phone call was finished. Never did the principal ever think that he would have to notify a whole classroom full of parents that their children had disappeared without a trace. Mr. Stern was still down there staring at that awesome hole, his practical, engineering nature not admitting yet what might have happened. "Well I can't help him," Mr. Reynolds thought. "I have to deal with the police, reporters and the F.B.I. Best I get to it."

# *An Unexpected Beginning*

\* \* \* \*

Mrs. Stern awoke with sunlight streaming into her face. Where was she? Stiffly she turned and stared out of the window. The classroom now rested at a slight angle in a clearing on the edge of a wide, slowly moving river. Beyond the river, in a reddish haze, appeared a vast, fertile valley, with a range of foothills; and beyond them distant mountains framed the horizon. Through the window near what had been the front door on earth, she could glimpse unfamiliar trees.

Restraining the impulse to dash out and explore immediately she realized her obligation to care for as best she could, the children who had become, through some quirk of fate, her sole responsibility. Caution was the important word now.

Quietly taking two P. E. flags and followed by two hungry cats she stepped out the door into the pleasantly warm sunshine. Rascal and Raquel immediately went off together into the strange forest. "I hope they find food as I can't help them, she thought. Standing momentarily to survey the scene she saw that the trees were quite like those she had known on earth. The foliage was different though. There seemed to be more clearing beyond the bushes close by, but nothing looked dangerous. Going into the underbrush a little way near some interesting rocks she tied a marker for the boys, then retracing her steps walked to the far corner of the building and marked a spot for the girls.

"Wake up everyone. We have some planning and exploring to do. I'm declaring a holiday from studies for a bit until we get settled."

Sleepy heads turned quickly into fountains of questions. Where are we? Will we stay here? Can we go outside? How will we live?  When do we eat?  Where's the bathroom?

"First things first!  Quiet!  We must be careful in a strange place.  I've gone out and picked two spots away from each other and as safe as I can see for now, to use as temporary bathrooms.  But first rule to remember: never go anywhere without a buddy.  It seems we are on a strange planet," explained Mrs. Stern.

"I don't believe that! scoffed Lee.

"It's true," chorused Ron, Stacy and Barry all at once.

"Gary, tell the rest of the class what you saw last night when I woke you to look out the window," she asked.  "And while he's doing that we'll risk opening some windows.  David, please open the lower windows for some ventilation.  Go on Gary."

"Mrs. Stern woke us up very quietly to look out and tell her what we saw.  She wanted to find out if we all saw the same thing.  It was only a quick look because we were moving so fast, but we saw the earth out there -- just as if we were standing on the moon."

Lee interrupted, "It probably was the moon, dummy!"

"No we saw North and South America just the way it is on our globe," Ron answered quickly.

"We can debate this later if we have to, but let's get on with our other plans.  Pick a partner and two at a time can visit our temporary bathrooms, Out the door behind me, boys look for the flag in the bushes on the left; girls go to the end of the building to the right and look for your flag. Russ, you and Jon take that clean bleach bottle down to the river, rinse it out, fill it and bring it back here as quickly as you can.

Chrissy, in the drawer, second from the sink are some half-pint, plastic juice bottles that I've saved to use for art.  There should be enough for each person to have one.  Pass them out. Those are the only ones we have so hang onto them. Use a crayon to put your initials carefully on the bottom."

"Thank you boys for getting the water. Pour a little of the water into Rascal's dish and see if he'll drink it. My, he was thirsty! We'll have to take a chance on it's being okay to drink. We haven't much choice. Pour a little in each bottle to rinse the dust out, then pour the rinse water in to the coffee can Jon is holding. Russ will fill your bottle up half way.

"Jenny while the boys are passing out water, give each person two more cookies."

Soon the brief snack representing breakfast had been finished. It wasn't much but it did help cheer everyone up a little. A class historian was elected to keep a day-by-day diary and permanent buddies chosen.

"Seeing to survival will help keep away the 'lonelies' at least," thought the teacher. "We'll keep busy so there won't be time to worry about missing our families."

"Hey, it's safe out here. I don't see any monsters. Can't we explore?" yelled red-haired Mark, as he burst through the door.

"In a bit, hold your horses," cautioned Mrs. Stern, "we still have planning to finish. While we are talking we should have look-outs to watch. I don't feel any danger but we must be prepared. Rick, you and Gary take the first turn, one at each door; just inside so you can hear us and watch at the same time. Leave the doors open for air."

"We will have to assume that we are never going back to earth and that what we have here is all we'll ever have except for what we get from our new environment. I guess we are pioneers in a way, so we must conserve wisely what we have. Therefore, no one is to use paper or pencils or chalk unless you are told to. We have to keep a diary of each day's events so if we make it as a new colony we'll have a history or if we don't and at some future time men from earth find this place they'll know what happened to us."

"We are lucky because we have encyclopedias with us to help with knowledge but at first we'll have to work with just the basics."

"What are the basics?  We have one already," questioned Mrs. Stern.  "Hilary?"

"Well we already have shelter if we count this room, but our cookies won't last long," answered Hilary.

"The third basic we have some of too but we'll need more eventually.  What is it? Troy?"

"Television!"

"Troy, that is not a well thought out answer," Mrs. Stern scolded. "Betsy?"

"We can't stay in these clothes forever.  What will we do to wash them?" Betsy replied.

"You're on the right track, Betsy.  Can you tell what the third basic is?"

"Soap?" suggested Betsy.

"No, Jeff?"

"More clothes?" guessed Jeff.

"Right, Jeff.  Food, clothing, shelter, the three basics needed for our survival.  I see that Rascal has solved his," said Mrs. Stern as the cat, followed by a delighted kitten, entered the room with a furry something in his mouth.

"Oh goody!  Our first monster," giggled Lee, wiggling up and down in his seat.

"Mrs. Stern, before he eats it maybe we should try to see what it is so we can get an idea of what lives in this place," suggested Jeremy.

"That's a good idea if I can persuade Rascal to let me look at it."

"Let me try," volunteered Tina. "Here Rascal, let me see," she coaxed. After some playful dodging and a small growl or two, Rascal gave up the limp body of his prize. His catch was a warm brown in color, not much bigger than a rat. Its furry face had a short stubby nose and the paws were not unlike Rascal's. The creature was not particularly meaty so as food for humans it might be too little to bother with.

"Boys and girls I suspect that for the time being we will have to become vegetarians. At least until we can arrange some means to kill game and to find those creatures we can eat safely.
Give Rascal his catch Tina. I hope he shares it with Raquel."

Rascal did just that. He seemed to realize that his life was suddenly different from what it had been. He readily became a hunter accepting that his humans couldn't provide for him. Rascal seldom seemed to stray too far. Eventually, he even became a weathervane, sensing rain before the children could see it coming. Whenever he chose to stay inside during the day they knew it would rain. Neither he nor Raquel slept out at night preferring to cuddle up to one of the children.

The friendly grey cat became very precious to the entire group, a poignant, living reminder of what had been left behind when they left Earth. Eventually he and Raquel presented their friends with enough kittens to allow each child to have a pet. Mighty hunters all!

"We are all anxious to look around and we do need to find some food sources quickly. After all the cookies are nearly gone. The water, fortunately, seems safe. With no visible signs of any other civilization as yet I doubt that we have to worry about pollution," commented the teacher.

"Let's stay together but all go out and look around on the riverbank between this building and the water. It's almost like a beach and gives a clear view of the area. Don't leave the clearing. We can't search in an unknown territory for someone foolish enough to stray out of sight."

Everyone was eager to explore. It was such a relief to be free of the classroom at last. The climate of this strange place seemed agreeable; warm, breathable air, running water.

"Hey, Mrs. Stern, where do I empty the garbage?" shouted Tom, waving the wastebasket.

"Tom! Don't throw away anything!" she ordered.

"Even smelly old apple cores?" he complained.

"Especially apple cores. Bring me the basket please. Boys and girls come here for a moment." When the children had gathered the teacher said, "We don't know about the seasons yet but we'll have to take a chance that the growing conditions will be right. We'll take the seeds from two of our apples and try planting them. The seeds from the third we'll try to save to plant elsewhere when we explore more later on. We'll do the same with the oranges. At least we'll know if earth things can grow here. As soon as we can we'll have to try planting the radish, corn and lima bean seeds I have for our science experiments. We might even plant the dried beans I use as counters for the math games. Let's decide where to plant the apples."

They finally chose a spot a little distance from the building where the forest was not too dense and for a short space, seemed flat and clear before the trees began. Holes were scooped out with flat stones for tools, several seeds placed carefully, covered with soil and then watered. A red poker chip glued to a large rock was placed near each planting to mark the spot.

Decision making in school was a game for grades. Now it really mattered. What they decided might mean the difference between safety or danger, food or starvation, even life or death.

Despite the fact that the children knew nothing of the climate or the soil, the apple trees grew well through the years that followed. They did get orange trees but not much fruit though they ate what the trees managed to produce.

Later they planted apple seeds as they explored and these trees provided well too. Tom once remarked that he hadn't expected to be Johnny Appleseed!

One of the hardest decisions to make was how to test possible food. It was finally decided that only two people at a time would test each thing and turns would be taken. That way the risk of everyone getting sick at the same time would be eliminated. The food search was to be scientific. Observe what "birds" and "animals" ate, especially Rascal. When trying something new, touch a bit to the tongue; if it stings, burns or tastes bad, throw it away. If not leave a little in the mouth for a few minutes. If nothing happens swallow and wait for an hour. If everything seems fine then try a small helping. No one was to test unless others were around to observe and record.

The kids were so hungry that this routine was hard to follow, but knowing it to be a very serious matter they stuck carefully to the plan.

Stacy and Hilary found some low bushes with curious, curly edged leaves growing near some rock outcroppings at the river's edge. Under the leaves they found something resembling red berries and volunteered to test them. Ron was to sketch and write a description of the bush and the berries while they waited for results.

Using some of the macramé string for a line and bending a hook from a paper clip with a flash of red material from the scrap bag, Mrs. Stern set David at the task of fishing. Jeremy was to help.

The rock outcropping jutted nearly to the water's edge, like a point, north of the beach-like area. Mrs. Stern and Mark followed the narrowed bank around the rocky point, picking their way carefully over the small, slippery stones. Here they found another small cove where the sun-warmed water was clear and quite shallow. The forest grew almost to the water, but several large, flat stones provided a welcome resting place.

"I think we can search safely in the water here for edibles. It's clear enough to see anything in the water that might approach to investigate us," Mrs. Stern said. "You sit on that rock there and I'll look around."

Just then their search was interrupted with a shout from Jeremy and they hastily returned to the others.

"David has something on the line. Look there!" Jeremy pointed. The water was indeed being thrashed about.

"I hope that twine holds if whatever it is on that line is edible," thought Mrs. Stern. "Bring it in carefully and steadily but as quickly as you can David. Russ stand by to help."

Gradually the struggling form was drawn out of the water.

"Yuk, what an ugly creature," commented Chrissy.

"Oh, poor thing," said Beth sadly.

Killing anything but offensive insects at home was unthinkable to her, but survival meant changing her ways, so while saying a silent apology to the innocent creature Mrs. Stern picked up a piece of driftwood and gave it a sharp blow on the head.

They saw that David's catch looked something like a large amphibian rather than a fish. Its froglike head and webbed forefeet were attached to a long, solid body much like a lizard. Its tail was sturdy and pointed and might have some use in swimming. The back limbs were large and powerful, jointed at the hip but shaped more like flippers. The skin was a mottled brown with orange cheeks and eye patches. The whole animal was about the size of a very large rabbit.

"Looks like something that is in the process of evolving or maybe between stages like a frog and a tadpole," Barry suggested.

"That's a good observation Barry," his teacher said. "Now we'll have to try and see if it's edible and decide how to prepare it."

"Jon, go get my desk scissors and the little jack knife I use to cut the erasers in half. They're in the top desk drawer."

Todd and I have collected a pile of wood for a fire. Should we start one?" asked Jeff.

"In a minute boys. It was a good idea to think of the wood. We'll have to build a fire pit with some stones so we have a protected cooking spot and something to rest food or utensils on. We can work that out later."

"Thanks for fetching the scissors Jon. Now watch while I take this creature apart and we can see if the life forms are like the ones we are familiar with in any way."

"Yeah, cut up the flizzard, I'm hungry," Troy ordered. Ever after that those creatures were flizzards to them all.

Carefully opening the abdominal cavity with the scissors proved to be a messy job. "Well we know the fluid resembles blood; apparently most of the organs are similar. Let's wash and clean those intestines, then stretch them out to dry. If they are strong enough we may find a use for them," commented the teacher as she continued the dissection.

Rascal and Raquel romped up eagerly so Mrs. Stern gave them each a piece of what appeared to be the liver. They ate it avidly and begged for more so she gave them each a tiny portion of the chicken-like flesh. This was readily accepted but they wouldn't touch the skin.

"We'll use that as a clue. I'd better skin it before we try to cook it."

"Boys, now you can try scooping out a fire pit. Line it with stones around the sides. Then try to get a fire going. I have one book of matches in my purse but we won't use them unless we have to."

"Since Rascal seems to think this is good to eat we can cook the flizzard. We might mold it in clay and set it on the ashes or poke it on sticks over the fire. We might even try frying it on that old cookie sheet I use for a paint tray. There seems to be enough fat on this animal. I think my being a pack rat is going to come in handy. Betsy, we might have enough TV dinner trays under the sink for each one to have a plate or at least to share. I'll try skinning this with my tiny jack knife. Never thought an advertising gimmick would come in so handy. We'll save the skin and try to dry it. It may be useful as leather."

"Stacy and Hillary have tested the berries and are O.K.," reported Ron.

"We gathered as many as we could find around here and we have half a can full," the girls said.

"They're good but awfully sweet. I don't think we can eat too many at a time," Hillary commented.

"Thanks girls for being the first to risk getting poisoned. If the berries are that sweet then we have enough for everyone to have a few for dessert."

The boys soon managed to have a cooking fire going with the help of a magnifying glass. When the coals were ready in the makeshift fireplace the flizzard fillets were quickly cooked on the cookie sheet greased with the flizzard fat. Rascal purred his way around hopefully and finally sat down to wait with his tail flipping impatiently, for a tidbit of the cooked meat. He was rewarded with a tiny taste and looked around for more, but of course there wasn't any. One flizzard didn't provide much of a meal for twenty-nine people but that and the berries did dull the hunger pangs somewhat.

"Now we have to think about cleanliness. Those berries were very sweet so rinse your mouths with water. Later we may find twigs we can use as brushes. Mark and I found a nice spot over there just beyond the point. The water is shallow and warm. Girls I want you to go and bathe. We don't have any soap but rinse off as best you can and leave your clothes on the bank. Rinse out your underwear and spread it on the rocks to dry. Someone will have to watch the water to guard against anything swimming into the cove that might be harmful. Take turns watching. I'll be there in a minute. Don't swim out into the river. In an hour or so the boys may have their turn."

"Boys, please gather more wood and pile it near the building. Be on the lookout for more berries or anything else we might eat."

By the time the bathing was done the day was mostly gone. Without artificial light living would now be regulated by the sun. As soon as it got near dark two more cookies apiece were handed out, sleeping arrangements settled and the diary updated. The teacher led the group in a few songs and all went to sleep. That is, most of them did.

Worry is the enemy of sleep and Mrs. Stern found herself wondering how she was going to manage being mother, father, teacher, doctor and provider for all her charges. They were too tired tonight to worry about missing their families, but what could she do to ease that pain. Wondering this she finally fell into a restless sleep with her head cradled on the scrap bag.

\*\*\*\*\*\*\*\*\*\*\*\*\*\*\*\*\*\*\*\*

Mrs. Thomas went about her routine of tidying up the kitchen after dinner, her thoughts occupied with Todd. She somehow felt he was very much alive, somewhere. The Air Force radar net had picked up a large unidentified flying object moving very swiftly on and out into space at the time the building disappeared. The shape was not that of any known craft.

"I can't help worrying, but I won't give up hope as some of the others have. There is more to this than we know about. I don't care if my husband thinks I'm crazy. It's got to be better than giving up," she said to herself as she wiped the stovetop clean.

# The Second Day

**\*\*\*\***

The first day had been a great adventure, but waking up hungry and realizing that food had to be found before eating, led to a gloomy beginning of their second day.

"I'd even eat boiled liver and eggplant," groaned Mark.

"I'm not THAT hungry yet," Betsy declared.

The gloom didn't even clear up when David and Jeremy came in with two more flizzards which they had thoughtfully decided to try for when they woke before the others.

"Is that all we're ever going to eat?" grumbled Michele.

"YOU could always volunteer to be our next meal," Lee suggested. "We'll pretend we're the Donner party".

"Ve-ree fun-nee," retorted Michele angrily.

"Hush! No family fights.  We all have to work at survival or we may not last long," cautioned their teacher. "We'll take turns doing things so we'll all know how.  Stacy and Jenny start the fire this morning.  Russ, Gary and Rick use my scissors and knife to clean and prepare the flizzards the way I did yesterday.  These look like fat fellows so save any chunks of fat and put them in one of those empty margarine tubs.  We'll find a cool place to store it to use for cooking.  Give the organs to the cats but try to cut them up first so they don't choke on the large pieces.

"While they're getting ready for breakfast the rest of you come with me.  See that meadow-like spot over there?  The forest seems to separate there so you can see the mountains beyond. I think we should try clearing that brushy, level ground and prepare it for planting."

"Stacy, when the fire and flizzard fillets are ready, ring my bell and we'll come back."

"Let's take these plastic bags in case we find any food."

The intended garden patch was just a short way from the building up a slight slope. The land leveled off into a small meadow. The ground was covered with many kinds of vegetation, all new to them of course, but nothing resembling grass. What struck them most was that things didn't seem to be very green. There were some yellow and blue blossoms but all the foliage seemed to have a reddish tinge as did the soil.

Mrs. Stern cautioned them as they walked to be careful where they stepped because all life forms would be unknown and would have to be approached with care.

"For my peace of mind I hope there are no snakes or spiders," she thought.

As they topped the rise and moved into the overgrowth the group was startled by a furious chortling sound and a flurry of activity somewhere nearby.

"Freeze", commanded Mrs. Stern. Let's go ahead slowly until we see what we've disturbed."

She often said she almost liked animals better than people. When no one was around to deride her actions Martha Stern talked at birds and beasts as though they were human. Thus from force of habit she thought, "Don't be frightened. We don't intend to harm you." The frantic chortling sound changed to a questioning trill and from a nearby bush several small heads peeped out.

"Oh look! Aren't they cute," Kristi said softly as she knelt to get a closer view of the strange creatures. With quick bobbling steps a little feathered being ran over and rubbed its head up and down Kristi's leg crooning softly as it did so.

"Guess we're going to be vegetarians," stated Tom. "Who could even think of eating something that lovable?"

"I could," answered Mike.

"Oh, there are more of them over there," Amy said pointing to a flock of birds emerging from the bushes. They came towards the group but stayed away from Mike. Their feathers were a shiny blue with soft buff colored downy chests. Slightly larger than Earth chickens with longer legs and slightly webbed feet, they crooned questioningly through beaks much like parrots.

"I wonder if they lay eggs or have live babies," asked Margaret.

"We'll have to observe them and see," Mrs. Stern replied. "It would be nice if they laid eggs. We could use them. I don't think I could kill one of these unless there was nothing else to eat."

Several of the hens ran over and settled near the teacher's feet and one boldly leaped high to settle in the crook of her arm. She stroked the soft feathers and it crooned to her, almost as a cat would purr. A larger bird, probably a male, stationed himself defiantly in front of Mike.

"Mrs. Stern-watch where you step," cautioned Ron. "One of our questions has been answered. Look!"

The little group of hens had moved off and where they'd been sitting were a half dozen brown, mottled eggs. Kristi's little friend had laid one in her lap!

What a help these will be for our food situation. "Thank you," she nodded at the chickens. "I hear the bell ringing, breakfast must be nearly ready. We'll have to come back to the gardening later."

They quickly retraced their steps to the campfire and shared the news of their find. Kristi's friend had followed and she was eagerly examined by the others. Mrs. Stern broke the eggs into the bleach bottle scoop and beat them with an old fork, formerly used for science. Using some of the flizzard fat she scrambled them on the cookie sheet. After a hungry Raquel ate the offered taste, the eggs were served with the fried flizzard. With the breakfast clean-up finished a class meeting was held to inventory what they had and discuss how it might be used. Everyone cleaned out their desks and cubby holes. In the process Troy discovered a nearly rotting potato he'd forgotten in the back of his cubby. It was supposed to have been for a science project. "Don't throw it away, we'll cut it up and plant it," said Mrs. Stern.

The list grew. Along with the plastic margarine tubs, yogurt cartons, assorted lids, aluminum TV trays, bleach bottle scoops, the cookie sheet, a cake rack, some glass jars, and the half pint plastic juice bottles each child had already been given, there were four foam cups from the teacher's cupboard, her tea mug, two dinner knives, an old steak knife, a fork and a tablespoon from a discarded set that Mrs. Stern had brought to school for the science sound experiments. Not much for kitchen equipment, but better than nothing. There were also a dozen or more two pound coffee cans with lids which held the stitchery yarn, eight small thermos bottles and twelve metal lunch boxes. Most of the children had backpacks which would help in food gathering.

Several of the desks yielded small, black plastic combs given out by the photographers when the yearly school pictures were taken, so some semblance of neatness could be maintained after all.

Metal, something they had taken for granted, was going to a problem. They had scissors, paper clips and a five pound box of small nails (for her class loom project), some staples for the stapler, three small nail files, a math compass, a few bobby pins, thumb tacks and straight pins and that was all. There was metal in their desks and the filing cabinet but converting any of it to tools or weapons was going to be difficult.

They were better equipped to make music with a piano, an autoharp, a set of bells, Todd's trumpet, Barry's violin, Amy's clarinet, and the flutes belonging to Michele and Margaret. Many of the children also had flutophones in their desks.

There was also a large quantity of cotton rug yarn they were using for stitchery and quite a varied assortment of leftover yarns and fabric scraps the parents had donated for art projects.

Mrs. Stern wondered if she could get the seeds to grow from the cotton boll Betsy had brought to her a while back to show the class.

Except for a few extra sweaters, jackets and dirty T-shirts some of the students had forgotten to take home, no one had a change of clothing. Several girls had shorts they wore under their skirts for P.E. thus giving them almost two outfits. Mrs. Stern took down the old pillowcase from the top of the cupboard in which she had stored the many pairs of discarded panty hose gathered from her neighbors and saved for art projects. She cut off the legs and gave each person a pair of the pants to use as a second pair of underwear. The boys protested vigorously and the girls fell over giggling but everyone finally settled down to write their names on the waistbands with a marking pen. What else was there to do about clothes at the moment? From the scrap bag the teacher would try to fashion new patchwork garments and mend the old ones until they could manage to find native materials to use. Already shoes and socks had been discarded except when away from the clearing.

"Our biggest problem is still food. I don't think we should consider moving away from here because we have the building for protection and a water supply nearby. There has to be some plan in our being here. I don't think it's entirely by accident. The whole thing is far too strange to be just a chance happening. So let's assume for now that we'll be able to get enough to eat if we look for it. We'll plant our garden, but weeks will go by before we can harvest anything. The radishes mature the fastest. If I'd known how important those seed packets would be I would have gotten more of a variety when I planned our science projects, the teacher commented ruefully.

"Mrs. Stern, aren't you afraid?" asked Chrissy.

"Oddly no. In a situation like this I suppose fear would be natural but I'm not afraid. In fact, at times I feel comforted though I can't explain that. I am worried about my great responsibilities; doing the right thing to keep us all healthy and alive. I do miss my own family terribly as I know you miss yours. But we haven't time to think much about that now. Let's get to work on the garden patch."

As they worked to clear a garden space they laid aside any foliage and roots they thought might prove edible. The boys carried stones to outline the boundaries of the plot. Using sticks they dug up and loosened the earth. Turning a chair upside down and using the top back piece as a sort of scraper, Michele and Annette smoothed off the surface. Half the radish and lima bean seeds were planted. One third of the corn because they would plant that at intervals. The potato was cut into five eyes and soaked in water for a while before planting. They had no idea if that was the right thing to do but since the potato looked a bit wizened it was hoped that a better chance for it's growing would come from soaking it first. Not all the seeds were planted. If the first planting didn't work out they'd have some to try again. Carrying water in coffee cans was tedious but necessary. They would have to find a better way and soon.

Bluebelle, as Kristi had named her, started to scratch at the newly planted rows. "No, no, ---shoo!" scolded Todd.

"I've noticed that these creatures seem to understand thoughts directed at them. Let's try something. Line up around the edge of our garden. Look at her and think of Bluebelle; think No! No! Don't eat in our garden."

It did seem silly but they tried it. It worked! Bluebelle didn't go in the garden nor did any of the other chickens.

While the garden plot was being readied, Mark, Tom and Jon helped Mrs. Stern build a sort of fish trap with the large wicker wastebasket. A little way upstream where a swift current swung near the shore they anchored the basket with sticks and stones to brace it in place. A large plastic bag with a hole at the end and tied around the top of the basket billowed inward with the rush of the water. Anything that went in through the top would find it difficult to swim back out.

"Hope we catch something. I'm tired of flizzard already," Jon commented.

Everyone worked hard so they were glad to stop and rest. A bath swim was ordered and this time the boys were first. Amy and Vicki volunteered to taste test some thick weed roots that looked like raw turnip.

"Tastes like celery, it's good," said Amy.

"Only a small bit, remember and we have to wait an hour," scolded Vicki.

There had been much of a low-growing, curly leaved plant that they had to pull out of the garden place. Michele and Annette thought it might be a substitute for lettuce but one tiny nip and it was so bitter Annette tasted it for hours.

Betsy and Margaret wading around near shore were having a contest to see who could squish up the most mud between their toes when they discovered some rough, roundish things that didn't seem to be rocks.

The girls gathered around while Betsy tried to break the thing open. No luck. Then their teacher tried to pry it open with the compass point. That didn't work either. As they stood there wondering what to try next the thing on the sand opened enough to extend a snail-like foot tentatively. Before the what-ever-it-was could dig itself into the sand or head for the water, Bluebelle had rushed up, slipped her beak into the crack and grabbed the thing inside the shell. Teetering slightly off balance she grasped the shell between her two feet and moving her beak back and forth in the crack of the shell, cut the muscle used to close it. The shell popped open but no one got to see what was inside because Bluebelle quickly ate the clam-like creature with great relish. She strutted around crooning with great delight over her treat.

"I think that might be something we will be able to eat if we can get them open," Mrs. Stern said. "Look for more of them girls."

Rascal had been watching from a distance and now he crept slowly and carefully toward Bluebelle. She watched his stealthy approach but instead of running away she ran at him, feathers ruffled, chortling a loud warning. Instantly it seemed, she was surrounded by her flock ready to do battle together against the hapless cat. Rascal sat down and meowed. He wasn't going to risk attacking a crowd! Most of the hens went back to the bushes for their afternoon siesta. The cats didn't seem inclined to bother them again.

The solar celery as they called it, tested out o.k. The girls found more of the rock clams and Barry agreed to test one raw, and Ron one that had been cooked. While the girls bathed Jon checked the fish trap but nothing was caught in it yet.

By late afternoon, tired and hungry, the children were ready to eat whatever was handy. They grumbled but ate the rock clams and the solar celery. Each had a cookie for dessert. The Girl Scout cookies would be rationed out as long as possible.

"While it is still light I want to rearrange the classroom so it will be more livable," said Mrs. Stern. "We'll set it up so there will be seven sleeping areas along the wall and under the windows with the rug in the middle for our living room. We'll use the tables and the bookcases as room dividers. I'll take the corner under the window with my desk and bookcase outlining my space." The tall bookcase, the science table and one of the low bookcases were used to make 'rooms' along the south wall. The back of the teacher's desk, the third bookcase and the reading table made two more spaces under the windows on the east wall. A table and the file cabinet defined the space under the chalkboard for the smallest group of three boys. The extra chairs were placed at the ends of the bookcases and the desks arranged around the edges of the rug. Now each small group had a place to call their own. In the succeeding weeks they would decorate their own spaces with Mrs. Sterns collection of posters and pictures from her picture file. Eventually beds and pillows would be fashioned from native materials.

Darkness settled in just as the last desks were shoved into place. This was the hardest time of the day where memories of home crowded in to bring sadness to them all. The thought of what to do had been troubling her ever since that first jolt hurled them into space. Food was hard to find but curing the hurt of being so abruptly taken away from their families was going to be even more difficult.

After the evening songs were sung Mrs. Stern said, "I've been wondering about the people we've left behind. There is only one way we can possibly let them know we are still alive and safe. It's very far-fetched but we'll have to try."

"Are you thinking of telepathy?" Ron asked.

"Yes. If we all concentrate at the same time everyday trying to reach the same person with the same message we might be able to reach across space. We might not. But at least there would be comfort in knowing we tried. I'm sure we are much in the thoughts of our families and before that fresh concern is blunted by time we should try to get through."

"It's silly. It won't work," scoffed Lee loudly.

"But it won't hurt to try it, will it?" Jeff said to Lee.

"Oh I'll try it if everybody else does," Lee agreed.

"You all know that Todd's house is right across the street from the school and I think you all know Mrs. Thomas. She is the one we'll try to reach first. I think that is the best choice because it is so close to where we started from.

"Todd you sit in the center of the rug and picture your mother in the kitchen. The rest of us will sit in a circle and hold hands and visualize Todd's house. Now do you have the house in mind?" the teacher said softly. "Think over and over; we are all alive and safe."

Every evening they repeated this ritual in the weeks that followed. Their concentration grew gradually so that it felt as if they were one in thought. Somehow it was comforting to them all.

# *Impossibly Probable*

****

For some time now thoughts of Todd always crowded into her consciousness, thoughts that seemed particularly strong every evening. "Maybe it's because I'm in the kitchen and we always talked about his day at school here," Mrs. Thomas reasoned. "I'm so tired maybe I'll just sit here for a moment before I unload the dishwasher. I miss the little guy so much." Wearily she sat at the kitchen table, rested her head against the wall and closed her eyes. Vividly a mental picture of her son leapt before her closed eyelids. He was sitting in the center of a circle of his classmates on the blue carpet used for the reading corner. Only the room had been rearranged. His eyes were closed and he seemed to be saying over and over, "we are all alive and safe". "I'm so glad to know that T.T.," she whispered fervently and he smiled.

*********************

Mrs. Hall cut across the playground on her way to room three where she worked as a volunteer mother-helper once a week. She wasn't surprised to see Mrs. Thomas standing silently at the roped off hole where room eighteen had stood. From her kitchen window she had often seen the parents of the missing children visiting that forlorn spot. Many seemed to be drawn there as if seeking the answer to the question of what had happened to a whole room full of people who had vanished into thin air without a trace.

"Morning Charlene. How are you doing these days?"

"O.K. during the days but I think I'm beginning to see things at night," Mrs. Thomas answered. Hesitantly she explained what had gone on the evening before. "I must be going a little daffy."

"I don't think I'd laugh at that. My grandmother used to tell us many strange things happen that we can't explain. Some I know are old superstitions but she was very wise and much of what she said made sense. I'll come over tonight and see if I can pick up any vibrations. It sounds to me as though they are trying to get through to us."

Todd's mother looked a bit worried. "You know I haven't mentioned this to anyone else because I don't want to be laughed at so please don't say anything," she begged.

"Don't worry, I won't risk my husband's laughing at my notions," Jeff's mother promised.

\*\*\*\*\*\*\*\*\*\*\*\*\*\*\*\*\*\*

Todd was smiling broadly with his eyes closed tightly. "She heard me. Mom heard me," he murmured softly.

"Don't anyone say anything," cautioned Mrs. Stern, "we'll have to check our impressions. Todd does your mother have a pet name for you?"

"Yes. But it's kind of silly so I don't want to say it."

"I don't want you to say it because I think that she called you by that name and if we all know then it's proof that we've gotten through. I'll write your nickname on a tiny piece of paper and fold it. Jenny will hold it without opening it. Each one will get the chance to whisper to me what they think they received as a message. Then we'll see if what I think I received matches the rest of your impressions. We'll ask Todd if that's it."

Jenny clutched the tiny scrap of paper used from their precious supply, while one by one the children whispered in their teacher's ear. Finally Mrs. Stern ended the suspense by saying "I think we all received the same message. Todd read what I wrote and see if that's your mother's favorite name for you."

By now the room was getting so dark that one of the few matches from Mrs. Stern's purse had to be used for Todd to see the writing. Everyone watched Todd closely through the darkening evening light as he read the slip of paper.

"That's mom's name for me," he whispered.

It was a wonderful feeling to realize that they had made a probable contact with Earth. At least someone knew they were still alive. Everyone went to sleep a little happier that night. In the following weeks the same time was set aside nightly for trying to communicate telepathically. Often they were discouraged, but gradually it seemed as though it became easier and that messages could be exchanged. Through the use of names, happenings and facts known only to one person on each side and transmitted to the group on either planet, proof of really sending telepathically was built up.

Perhaps it was only clutching at any shred of hope that led Mrs. Hall into trying with Mrs. Thomas to contact her son but in the end she was more than glad of her belief that such things could happen. At first the two mothers kept it to themselves, but as the days passed and they felt more sure of their contacts they asked a few more of the mothers to join them. Before long the daily evening meetings became so noticeable from the parked cars and obvious activity that the carefully kept secret broke into the news, first as a hint in a well-known gossip column then later by a TV station. When Mr. Stern received the right answer to his question about his mother's unusual middle name, he finally believed the contact was a true one.

The news of such a happening electrified the world. As usual with this kind of thing everyone wanted to get in on it. Scientists wanted to set up research projects, psychics claimed to be receiving messages of their own, magazines, newspapers and television stations wanted exclusive rights to all new messages. It finally became necessary to set up an office and hire a lawyer to handle all the many details. A portable classroom was rented and parked next to where room eighteen had been. This became the office and the evening meeting place. Mrs. Thomas was then able to call her home her own again!

# *Forest Roaming*

****

The work of staying alive made the weeks fly by. The first radishes came up and the other plants seemed to be coming along nicely; especially with Bluebelle and her friends to stand guard over the precious garden patch. Gradually other food sources were developed, mostly greens of different types. A large, slow animal like a ground hog or giant mole seemed plentiful. When several boys trying out their hand at crafting bows and arrows accidentally killed one, they found it to be very good to eat. The improvised fish trap eventually caught several kinds of fish and a type of eel. Being hungry was an effective antidote to picky appetites so anything on the day's menu was always eaten. Bluebelle's friends obliged by laying eggs with great regularity in a little brush hut next to the building.

As closely as they could judge, if there were seasons, the group had landed in the very early spring. The days had grown longer and somewhat warmer. Different little flowers had appeared. The boys and girls laboring to dig the holes and carrying the stones for the pits beneath the permanent outhouses they were constructing, complained of the heat more loudly and frequently. Digging was difficult with the shovels crudely made from the seats of some of the classroom chairs. It was fortunate that the soil was not tightly compacted.

After Annette swam cautiously out into the river, swimming was allowed at least to the middle of the stream. The children were really thriving, Mrs. Stern thought as she watched them at their tasks one morning. All were tan and fit it seemed. Amy had even gotten a wee bit fatter. The pain of separation from their families had been eased by their nightly communications. With one or two children being the focus point each evening everyone felt they had gotten through.

With the food problem under control some thought could be given to exploring more of their new surroundings. The first hike took place on a Sunday. They were keeping the calendar as they would on Earth and Sunday was their day for rest and fun.

Their first trip was planned for a hike in the forest behind the building. They had already gone part way into the trees to set up the outhouses and to look for the firewood they used, but no one had gone much farther than the first mile or two though it was always tempting to go just a bit farther each time.

Everyone took their school book bags or bags woven from reeds in case food was found or some other useful thing. Betsy carried a roll of bright roving yarn and a pair of scissors. At intervals along the trail they stopped to tie a marker on a branch high enough, it was hoped, to be seen but not brushed off by any passing animal.
Bluebelle and Rascal joined the party but Raquel stayed behind with her first batch of kittens.

The first part of the trail was familiar so they passed through the brush and into the deeper part of the forest. Here the trees were larger and the undergrowth less dense. It was also cooler which was very welcome for the day promised to be very warm. Here the reddish tinge on the foliage they had noticed before didn't seem to be evident. Everything was a lush shade of green. Underfoot was a deep carpet of moss that muffled their footsteps and provided a comfortable cushioned effect as they walked.

A flash of bright yellow drew gasps of delight. A bird! Up until now none except the space chickens like Bluebelle had been seen. They'd only caught a glimpse of this new species but at least they knew birds existed here. They were careful to watch and listen as they went along.

Here and there where shafts of sunlight filtered through the foliage wild flowers grew in perfumed profusion. The pioneers were lucky enough to find clumps of their sweet berries. Stopping to pick those gave Rascal a chance to rest and Bluebelle a chance to scout for tidbits.  Kristi keeping a motherly watch on her pet's wanderings found Bluebelle drinking at a little spring.  This was a great find, as all were thirsty.

Bluebelle was a great help that day for while digging around in the humus under the trees near the spring she exposed some thick tubers which they took back with them.  Baked in the coals of the fire the tubers smelled delicious and tasted almost like a crunchy baked potato.

Refreshed with a drink of cold water and a handful of berries they moved on and up a slight slope where the hardwood trees gradually thinned out and were replaced by a kind of fir.  The branches grew so close to the ground and near each other from tree to tree that it seemed an almost impenetrable wall of greenery.

"We'll never get through here." Mark complained.

"Let's not give up, we may be coming to an ocean.  I think I hear waves breaking," urged Ron.

"You may be right, Ron," Martha agreed.  The more formal Mrs. Stern had been dropped when she discovered the situation appeared to be permanent.  "We'll follow along the edge of these trees to the left and maybe there will be an opening."

"We could break off some of the lower branches and force our way through," suggested Jon.

"Those branches look too thick and strong to do that," scoffed David.

"I wouldn't try it.  Look at Rascal and Bluebelle.  They could squeeze underneath but they seem to shy away from those branches," Kristi noticed.  "Maybe they are kind of poisonous."

"Probably man-eating trees like the Venus flytrap plant that eats flies at home," gloated Lee gleefully.

"More like Poison Oak I'd say," Tom commented.

"How's the yarn supply Betsy?" asked Martha. "Now's not the time to run out."

"Oh we can go for a while longer yet," Betsy answered.

The group kept on going along the strange border of trees, drawn by the sounds of what must be an ocean. They had agreed to turn back at noon so there would be plenty of time to get back to home base before darkness fell, but there didn't seem to be any harm in going just a little bit farther. So they pressed on. Soon they felt that maybe the trees on their left were thinning. The ground seemed to slope downward a little.

Suddenly they were stopped! They had walked into a gully with a sheer wall of rock at the end. They couldn't go forward and that tantalizing surf sound seemed so close! To their left the menacing fir trees marched single file almost to the rocky wall.

The forest to the right seemed to curve back the way they'd come.

"Oh look, I think we can squeeze through right there where the sun is peeking through," Beth pointed. The trees didn't quite touch the rock and the sun did appear to shine a path to the other side.

"I'll try it," Amy volunteered, "I'm small enough to slip through." Quickly she moved forward, scrambled up the slight slope and inched her way past the tree branches.

"Oh there is an ocean and it's beautiful!" Amy cried. Before Martha could warn the others to be careful all the children had followed Amy through the opening so there was nothing to do but slip past the trees herself. Rascal and Bluebelle refused to go anywhere near the trees.

"Just wait here and we'll be back", the teacher consoled the lonely pets.

Stretched before them at the base of the cliff was a glittering blue ocean. It's vastness reached the horizon without the break of islands or vessels of any kind. They were standing on a rocky point with no visible way down to the sandy beach below.

"We'd better start back. As it is we may not get home before dark now, we've taken so much time," scolded the teacher. But when they turned to squeeze back through the opening it was no longer there! The tree branches had pressed against the rock.

A quick search in the fading light didn't turn up any safe way down to the beach. They were trapped!

"We'll have to wait until morning now. Maybe the light then will show us a way. The shadows at this time of day can be very deceiving. If we sit down against the boulders here at the end of the point, close together, we'll be sheltered against the offshore breeze. Try to get some rest all of you," she ordered.

"What about the communication tonight?" asked Jeff.

"It will be a good chance to see if we can send from another spot. But we don't want to alarm our people back home. Let's send "on forest camp out, found large ocean'," Martha suggested. Evidently the worry got through any way. The message came back, "Worried- take care". Sometime during the cold, damp night Martha was awakened by a moist nose rubbing against her cheek.
"Rascal!" she whispered. "How did you get here?"

A strange half-light somewhat like moonlight seemed to be shining though no other planet was visible in the night sky. Looking toward the frightening tree border she saw a strange sight. All the branches were folded up quite like giant buds. Perhaps they could get through the barrier now. Waking the children gently and cautioning for silence she followed Rascal forward, the children in single file behind her. Even though the opening between the trees seemed wider the brave cat stuck close to the rock wall they had slipped past earlier. They all got through just in time. Jon was the last and the branches had started to swoosh down just as he reached the rock face. He stumbled and fell but Jeremy grabbed his hands and pulled him along on his belly. The tip of a branch grazed the sole of his shoe. It started to disintegrate! Jon shook the shoe off quickly.

"It's hot!" he screeched, hopping along to join the others.

"Look at my shoe. It's ruined," he mourned.

"At least you're safe" Martha said gratefully. "Those branches seem to be highly acid. No wonder the animals were so cautious. Brave boy Rascal, thank you," as she gave him a scratch under his chin. "I think the movement of so many of us past the trees brought the branches down. I'd guess they fold up at night to fool possible prey into passing between them. Let's try to back track while we can still see a little by this 'moonlight'. I'd feel safer away from those trees."

Tired as they were, everyone was glad to follow that suggestion so they stumbled along until they reached the spring they'd stopped at earlier. Here everyone settled down wearily and slept soundly until the sun came up and Bluebelle's cheery chortling woke them.

# Will We Ever Reach the Beach?

**\*\*\*\***

After their near misadventure no one was too eager to explore for several days after that. It really was the most unpleasant thing that had happened to them so far. The days were hard because they had to keep working for food and firewood, but life on the planet was not inhospitable; in fact often quite pleasant under the circumstances.

Perhaps they had become too complacent about danger. This experience as frightening as it had been served to remind them how necessary it was to keep alert. Soon however, the remembrance of that shining ocean beckoned strongly and the children talked of finding another way to reach it.

"The river must eventually reach the sea," reasoned Barry. "So why don't we follow it?"

We could build a raft and float down," suggested Jeff.

"That would be too hard to do without saws, dummy!" countered Mike.

"Not only that, but a raft large enough to hold all of us would be very difficult to handle. We know nothing of the depth of the river, rapids or outcroppings of rock, hazards like that," Martha mentioned. "We could try exploring along the river bank. It won't be as easy as walking in the forest and more dangerous because of possible injuries climbing over slippery rocks and such."

In the end, after much discussion it was agreed to try following the river the next Sunday.

This time the difficulty of the trip was almost reversed. Where going in the forest was fairly easy until they met the poison trees, walking along the riverbank was difficult from the first. Boulders had to be climbed or waded around. The damp rocks were slippery so a fair share of bruises were gathered by several of the boys and girls.

At one point the banks on either side narrowed and the river became faster and deeper as it rushed through the gorge. They thought at first there wasn't a way to get through, but by retracing their steps for about a half a mile and then climbing the steep bank they were able to work their way along through the overgrowth until they reached the top of the gorge. Gazing down at the swift river running below they could see the rapids at the farther end of the canyon. So much time had been wasted by the necessary back tracking that they could go no further that day. Instead they turned back to camp, this time working their way along the top of the bluff and through the forest. It was well that they did because one of their more fortunate discoveries was made.

Just before the bluff dipped down gently to a more level bank they came to a sunny spot with low lying bushes curving into a protected cul-de-sac. Michele spied some unusual yellow flowers and went to investigate.

"Come see what I've found," she called.

"Do you think they're good to eat?" asked Stacy.

Everyone crowded around to look at the many cantaloupe sized fruit which nested in circles of leaves. They looked quite heavy but were kept from falling to the ground by the rough gray branches. Large, heavily scented blossoms were a deep yellow with a lighter yellow trumpet and long red stamens.

"Smells kind of lemony."

"Wonder if that's a squash type or a melon?"

"Hope it's good to eat. We could stand something new on our menu."

"Well there's only one way to find out boys and girls."

Rough spears made of one half of a pair of scissors honed sharp on a rock and fastened to a strong, light weight staff had been made by most of the boys. Rick used his to cut open the melon-like fruit. There was an immediate gush of a tasty smelling juice. The inner cavity was filled with seeds tightly packed, not unlike pumpkin seeds. The fleshy part was as yellow as the blossoms and tinged with the same red as the stamens. Jeff, the taster this time, declared his first nibble delicious, lemony and sweet. It was hard to wait for the possible poisonous results but they did. Each one gathered two or three of the new fruit to carry and found them surprisingly light.

The melons proved to be very versatile. They kept well, so could be gathered and stored. They were light to carry and became a staple trail food. The juice could be used as it came from the melon or added to water to make a refreshing drink much like lemonade. For a group of children used to all kinds of soft drinks this was definitely a relief from nothing but water. The seeds could be toasted and eaten, or best of all, when ground in a makeshift mortar made a very useful flour from which they made tortillas, bread, and a kind of cake sweetened with the juice of berries.

Melon fruit was delicious as is or cooked into a sauce. The rind halves when cleaned of their insides and dried in the sun were waterproof, making good bowls. Mark even managed to make a fairly good kickball of sorts, by cleaning one of the melons out through a small hole, and waiting impatiently for days for it to dry and stuffing it lightly with dried grass. He glued a patch over the hole with rubber cement and his creation was finished.

If any were inclined to be disappointed by not reaching the ocean that day, it was quickly dissipated by finding the new fruit.

Free time that week was used to clear and mark a trail paralleling the river along the top of the bank so they could get to the melon patch and reach their stopping place. Then they could get a faster start to their exploration the next Sunday. Everyone was set for a very early start so sure were they that they would reach their goal. At first light Hilary woke them all. After a hasty melon breakfast they started out. The path was now familiar at least as far as the melon patch for it had been well traveled in just a week. The going from there to their last stopping point the previous Sunday, was a little slower as they toiled upward over the rocky way to the plateau.

Looking down into the gorge where the sparkling, deep river rushed between the sheer rocky walls was quite a dizzying experience.

"If we can manage to get to the other side of this gorge somehow, I bet we could put a bridge across here someday," remarked Ron.

"Come on, worry about that later. We want to get to that ocean," urged David.

After clambering around, over and through the jumbled rocks blocking easy passage they finally glimpsed the ocean stretched out ahead of them. It was a beautiful sight.

They were disappointed however, if they thought reaching the beach was going to be easy. There the sandy beach was, stretched out below them temptingly, but there seemed to be no way down. The determined band began a painstaking search along the cliff edge. There appeared to be a natural ramp down the cliff face at one point, but the way to it was blocked by several gigantic boulders.

"Maybe there is a good reason for our not being able to get to the beach. Remember the trees? They were almost like a hedge. Now our way is blocked again. We'd better be very cautious. I think all we can do today is try and clear the way to the beach."

Secretly Martha was puzzled and alarmed. Her instincts told her something wasn't quite right. It was almost as though they were purposely penned in. Why? While the boys and girls tried to move some of the rocks blocking their way down the teacher paced the bluff and watched the horizon. Somewhere there had to be a clue for their being here. She was certain they were being observed but how? By whom? Until she reached some conclusion she wouldn't bring it up to the children. So far they were as happy and healthy as they could be under the strange circumstances. There was excitement in the exploring of a new planet, with much to see and do as well as the problems of survival which up to now they had managed well enough. Perhaps the natives of this planet were testing them to see if earthlings would survive. What better choice than children who had not yet been taught to be warlike.

"Well that's just a guess. I'm not even sure there are 'others' on this planet," Martha mused. "Come on kids. We've got to start back," she called.

# *Disaster*

Despite her vague misgivings they went back again and again to see if the rocks barring the way might somehow be moved. One of the more pressing reasons was their need for salt. If the ocean was indeed that and not a vast fresh water lake they might be able to set up a way to evaporate the water for salt.

Ron had been studying the ramp as carefully as she had and one day voiced his opinion to his teacher that he felt the ramp was not natural. "Someone or something made it I'm sure," he said.

"If we manage to move those stones we'll get the chance to look at it more closely. Probably sooner. Look at Gary and Rick." The two boys had dragged a sturdy sapling from the forest and with the help of the others were trying to lever one of the boulders away from the pile blocking their way.

Mark gleefully added his weight to the pole and little by little that first boulder moved away. Before returning to camp that day they removed another. Everyone was so tired they dragged wearily back but not before stopping to gather melons on their way.

Try as they would the last and largest boulder could not be budged.

"Boys and girls, it was meant to be there for a reason. I think to prevent us from getting to the beach. Whether to protect us or to protect some other being from us I don't know. I think we must proceed with great caution. We can build a dirt ramp to the top of the boulder and then by wedging logs between the stone walls on either side of the rock blocking us and filling the crevices with earth, build a stairway down to the ramp."

"Why not just build a ladder of vines we can pull up in a hurry if we have to," asked Russ.

"That's a good thought but a ladder like that might collapse if we all tried to get up it at once. In case of a hasty retreat enough of us couldn't get up and over in a hurry. And if we want to carry food and such from the beach below it would be easier on steps instead of a ladder," Martha replied.

Though they grumbled at the hard work and her caution, the group set to work building the ramp and the crude stairs. Everyone gathered sacks of pebbles and small stones to build the ramp. Soil was heaped on top and trampled down. Finding logs was harder. This was eventually made easier when makeshift machetes were painstakingly fashioned from some of the l-shaped seat bracings taken from the backs of the desk chairs. Hours of rubbing the metal against rock put a rough cutting edge on the tool.

Every spare minute went into the project. Twice they camped overnight on Saturday to get an early start on the work Sunday morning.

Getting the ramp on their side to the top of the huge boulder was completed fairly easily. Reaching that goal gave them a lift. Building the log stairway on the other side was tougher. A stout post had been set in place upright against the boulder as the ramp was built and the rocks and earth held it securely in place. Now using this as an anchor, materials and workers were lowered to the other side.

David and Jon were the first to be let down on the vine ropes. They had to resist the temptation to race down to the beach but it had been agreed that no one would go unless all of them did. When the braided vines held the boys, several others were lowered to join them and the first logs were wedged in place. The work on the stairway had begun. Lookouts were posted to keep watch and changed regularly so everyone shared tasks evenly.

It was Gary who while on watch pointed out that no one had

noticed any real tidal action. The level of the waves on the beach always seemed to stay the same.

"Perhaps the tide changes at night or maybe there aren't tides because we really haven't noticed a moon," Martha suggested. "We'll have to watch more closely."

At last the rudimentary steps were finished. Everyone climbed up, over and down, gathering in a small cluster at the base of their stairway before proceeding carefully to the beach.

The sandy ramp down led between unbroken rock walls curiously smooth to the touch. Once past their boulder barrier it was almost like walking down a cattle chute or open roofed subway tunnel. The only way out was down or back the way they had come.

Emerging at the base of the cliff the shining sea in front of them, was a breathtaking moment. The air here was pleasingly warm and moist. The beach was much wider than it appeared from above. It stretched unbroken for miles in a shallow crescent before reaching the horizon on either side. The water was indeed salty and warm but curiously devoid of any life that they could see. Cautious exploration for a short way showed the vast cliff unbroken by crevices or caves, nor a boulder on that perfect beach, except where the river tumbled from its imprisonment in the narrow canyon. Its swift course acted as an impassable barrier to the stretch of sand beyond the far bank.

"Wall number three," murmured the ever serious Ron.

The excitement of finally reaching the ocean died down quickly as all felt the disappointment of finding another barrier to easy exploration of their strange, new home. Except for the salt water and the view nothing else had been gained for all that struggle. There didn't seem to be any new food sources either.

Suddenly an overwhelming rush of panic hit Martha. Something seemed to be shrieking silently, imploringly, inside her head. Danger! She whirled quickly searching. Had someone called?

Run!  To the cliff!"  No one had said anything she was sure.

Turning to ask Ron if he had felt the same clear warning she saw that he was already running toward the cliff.

At that moment Troy remarked, "Hey somebody sure pulled the plug. Look at that ocean!"

The gentle, steady roll of waves had changed.  Already there was a wide stretch of damp sand growing ever wider by the second as the water receded with spectacular speed.

Run! Run back!" Martha screamed.  Blowing her whistle frantically, she stirred the group into rapid retreat.  Rick raced out in front passing Ron quickly.

"Tina, Mike, move!  Run for your life!" Martha ordered.  She grabbed Amy's hand and dragged her toward the ramp.

All of them reached the base of the cliff quickly enough but running up the steep incline was not so easy.

"Keep moving, we're not out of danger yet.  Get going!" the breathless teacher urged.

"I'm tired.  I can't keep going," Amy wailed and sat down.

Yanking her to her feet, Martha gasped at Amy, "Unless you want to drown in a tidal wave you'd better keep moving and fast!"

Mark kicked her as he went by.  "Get going!!"

Gasping for breath, tripping, sliding bumping into each other, the frantic children toiled swiftly upward.  Ron, Rick and Hilary reached the top first and helped drag the others over as they reached it.  Midway in the panicky dash the queer silence was broken by a growing, thundering roar which added impetus to their fearful flight.

Just as the last of the group reached the bottom of the steps, the cliff shook and the noise became unbearable. The stragglers were hit by a giant jet of water rushing madly through the narrowed walls of the ramp way and catapulted through the air to land in a jumbled heap several feet away in a clump of dripping brush.

Seconds passed, though it seemed much longer, before the stunned, gasping children dared to move. Martha, soaked and battered, pulled herself up from the bush she had fallen into as the weakening column of water had poured past her over the boulder. "Are we all o.k.? Let's round everybody up and take a head count."

A pained groan drew their attention to the crumpled heap of muddy bodies in the dripping bushes. Eight stragglers had received the brunt of the giant water jet. Troy had been barely ahead of it so he was shoved along by the very beginning of the wave as by a giant shovel. Luckily he was only bruised and scraped. The others had not fared so well. Mike, Lee, Jeff, and Todd had been gathered up as they chugged doggedly along the last few feet to safety, and slammed into a balled up knot of twisted limbs. Lee gasping for breath had landed on Jeff who was unconscious. Mike was bleeding from a mouth cut and Todd was in speechless shock. Worst of all no one could find Tina or Amy.

A frantic search began. The stairway was demolished! A bright patch of cloth led to Tina who had been wedged under some of the falling logs and nearly drowned by the receding water. Miraculously except for the fright and several serious cuts, Tina was all right when they freed her from her temporary prison.

While carefully untangling and tending to the injured boys, Amy was found beneath the unconscious Jeff, her leg broken.

Facing any disaster is difficult enough but coping with injuries without medical aid or supplies and no hope of any, is especially frightening.

After a careful check it appeared that Jeff had escaped broken bones except for a possible skull fracture, so four of the boys carried him carefully to the shade of the nearest tree where Lee and Troy sat resting. Margaret led the dazed Todd over to the group and stayed to watch them, especially Jeff. The rap on his head was sure to make him ill if he moved around too much after regaining consciousness.

Wasting not a drop, Michele and Stacy used some of the drinking water they carried on hikes, to wash off Tina's cuts. One was very deep and binding it would not be enough. Martha was forced to stitch it with the needle and thread in the work bag she always carried. Daylight hours had to be used for sewing and the patchwork clothing needed to keep her large brood clothed. Now some of those same scraps hoarded from the dwindling art project supplies were used instead for bandages.

She'd read somewhere that there was less pain involved if cuts were sewn up right after the injury but it didn't make it any easier for Tina or the teacher who had never done such a necessary treatment before. There was so way of sterilizing anything, nothing to use but water. Hilary and Kristi helped to hold and comfort Tina who really did well through the ordeal.

Amy's leg presented the worst problem of all. The break appeared to be below the knee. It would have to be set if she was not to be crippled. Very carefully, step by painful step, the groaning girl was carried into the shade and settled gently on the ground. Before touching the injured leg Martha felt the other leg to see how the bones were positioned. Then to make sure she checked Beth's and Vicki's too.

Gingerly she probed the injured leg while Amy tried not to cry. Finally knowing she had to do something, Martha reluctantly moved the bones into place as best she could while several of her friends held the screaming little girl still. Several straight saplings were tied around the leg with dried flizzard gut to brace it. Jeff had come to and was asking over and over for his mother. Betsy was doing her best to quiet him down.

"We can't move Amy or Jeff yet and several of the rest of

you are not in such good shape either. I'm afraid we'll have to stay here tonight." Several of the swiftest hikers were sent back to get food and jackets to cover the wounded, as well as a shelf from one of the bookcases. Hilary and Stacy went to the river to refill the water bottles. For the moment nothing more could be done.

"Betsy I need a few moments alone to think," the worried Martha said. "I'm going over to the edge of the cliff but I won't be far. Call me if you need me."

"O.K., I'll watch the patients," assured Betsy.

Now that the worst part of the crisis had passed the awesome burden for her charges returned even more heavily. In the need to care for the injured children there hadn't been time to think of the consequences. Had she done the right thing with Amy's leg? What could she do if infection set in? What about Jeff's head injury?

Her agitated pacing led her to the cliff's edge where she sat down wearily to contemplate the ocean below. The water, while still churning, had returned to near normal level. Gazing at the steady wave action was somehow soothing.

The rock barrier had obviously been put there purposely as a protection, of this she was sure now. Some intelligent being had done it, but had not destroyed the ramp way. Was this a seasonal occurrence? Maybe it was safe at times to go to the beach, but wouldn't the natives be aware of that? The rocks must have been put there to protect the unsuspecting. And that clear warning of danger; where and from whom had it come? She'd have to check with Ron and compare reactions.

Her idle gaze followed the dipping, whirling flight of seabirds hovering above the now peaceful sea. Sea birds! Where had they come from? The curious lifelessness of the beach which they had found so ominous and depressing had changed. Perhaps the giant wave had something to do with that.

Hurrying back to the casualties Martha urged Betsy,

Margaret and Annette to go and see for themselves how the beach seemed to have been transformed.

Daylight gave way to the shadows of evening just as the tired children who had gone for supplies came trudging up the now familiar trail. A fire was lit and a quick meal prepared while Jeff, Tina and Amy were made as comfortable as possible. Lee was sore all over, but except for the bruises he appeared to be fine and already regaining his good humor. Their communication home that night was met with sympathy and encouragement.

The next morning after a restless night Jeff seemed a little better. At least he knew where he was. He was too heavy to carry and though he should be resting he was helped slowly down the trail with frequent stops, back to the classroom. This took nearly all day. Once there he was made to rest for several days, with light tasks for a while after that.

Meanwhile, Amy, her leg cradled with the big pillow from the reading rug was strapped to the bookcase shelf which barely accommodated her small body. Groups of four took turns carrying her as carefully as possible, back to camp. It was a slow painful process for her but they finally got Amy back and bedded down. About all that could be done for the pain was cool, wet compresses on the foreheads of both Jeff and Amy. Martha rationed out, as long as they lasted, the few aspirins she had in her desk, giving them to Amy at bedtime. It did seem to aid her sleeping, little as it was. In the days that followed the leg was carefully re-splinted as the swelling went down. The boys got together and fashioned crutches from some sturdy branches and Amy was able to move about a little, very gingerly.

Tina's cuts healed, miraculously without infection though not without scars.

The most surprising sight greeted them that first morning back at camp after the accident. The whole flat plain across the river was flooded, looking much like a vast, very shallow lake. In a day or two this was gone but as it receded the whole area became alive with a new growth of plants and flowers, along with a fluttering, twittering mass of many birds and insects. The river seemed to be filled with fish of many new varieties making food gathering a much easier task.

Seasons on their new planet seemed to change with dramatic swiftness and effects.

# *Mountain Mystery*

****

The disaster date was noted as well as the subtle signs leading up to it so that the pioneers were able to avoid the beach when the great wave was due. Because the other stones had been removed, the force of the water had dislodged the remaining boulder somewhat, making it possible for that last large piece of the barrier to be removed. With the way to the ramp cleared easy access to the beach was assured. It became a favorite place to hunt for eatables and colorful shell forms which the children made into jewelry or specimen collections.

After several dismal tries the boys and girls managed to build a canoe of sorts to cross the river and explore the verdant marsh. Though the marsh yielded lush grasses for soft bedding and some new foods they were unable to go very far across it because of the treacherous mud and possible quicksand.

The weeks slipped by into months and finally years. Study skills were worked at regularly so they wouldn't be forgotten. The storybooks and readers had been all but memorized, the encyclopedias very familiar. After much experimentation a rough paper was developed from the marsh reeds so some writing and drawing could be allowed though the supply of carefully hoarded earth paper and composition books was nearly gone. As soon as it was gone the diaries they were keeping in tiny script, would be written on the blank pages and margins of the encyclopedias.

The amateur farmers had learned to save enough seeds from their carefully tended gardens to plant the next crop. The corn and potatoes were particularly successful. Even cotton was produced from that one sample boll and eventually some crude cloth was woven on backstrap looms copied from illustrations in a book about American Indians.

With dried fish, stored melons and potatoes the leaner winter season was passed more easily. Some of the boys and girls constructed small cabins of their own near by, furnishing them with handmade chairs and beds with marsh grass mattresses and pillows, though the former classroom remained the central meeting place and main shelter for most.

The need to explore was always present, especially the mystery of what lay beyond the mountains which seemed to fence them in on one side with the ocean on the other. The range curved in a giant crescent eventually reaching into the sea with vast, unclimbable cliffs and churning waves where they met the sea, permitting no passage beyond.

The danger alert felt by both Martha and Ron had been discussed many times as well as the obvious telepathic communication in simple ways with some of the animal species like Bluebelle. The very fact of their being there was so incredible that it had to be a managed event not a chance happening. All came to feel that the answer lay beyond the mountains. They must get past them somehow and the only way not tried yet was through the deeply forested lands between them and the mountains.

Following the river toward the mountains proved to be a dead end though a beautiful one. After toiling for days over rocks, through brush and brambles, following the river which became ever narrower, deeper, and swifter they came to a magnificent waterfall near the base of the foothills. When they reached the top of the falls, a deep blue lake spread before them like an uncut sapphire. The spot was breathtakingly beautiful. This proved to be the source of the river, supplied they supposed, by underground springs as exploration around the lake didn't turn up any springs feeding into it. The discouraged explorers built a base camp at the lake and a better trail for hauling supplies to be stored there from the home place now referred to as Outer California.

By now all were seasoned woodsmen capable of surviving on their own. The ceaseless search was well organized into smaller parties systematically exploring from the base camp. One team always remained at Outer California to tend the gardens and care for the pets. Rascal and some of his offspring always prowled along the trails with the searchers.

At the end of the third year the most direct route had been marked into the foothills with food caches spaced every forty miles. They estimated a long day's hike at nearly twenty miles, making the distance approximately three hundred miles to the brooding, mysterious mountain range.

Exploration from now on would mean more difficult climbing and searching for a pass through the mountain barrier. As soon as the spring planting in the fourth year was completed a larger expedition was organized. The ropes and climbing clothes they had worked on all winter along with the sun-dried foods prepared as light-weight trail provisions were all packed for the two week trek to their farthest camp. Additional food supplies were stashed in caches along the way for use when foraging was poor.

One team was to remain behind as usual to keep things going at the home base and to maintain the nightly communications with Earth. Experimentation had proven that the telepathic messages would work between teams if they tried at special times, though small groups could not reach Earth except from Outer California.

Amy's leg had healed surprisingly well but she could not keep up on long forced hikes, nor did Martha want her to risk breaking it again in a possible fall while climbing, so Amy was to remain behind. Vicki tired quickly so she stayed too with Beth, Tina, Mike Lee and Jeff, filling out the rest of the support team. The three boys would take more supplies later to the two nearest camps with the help of a clever cart Lee had devised.

Excitement grew as the preparations for this trip were completed. Everyone hoped that this time some answers to the mystery of their landing here would be found beyond the mountains.

The trek by the well-seasoned hikers to the foothills was

made in record time over the familiar trail, and a base camp quickly set up. Scaling the mountains would be the last resort because of the risk. Without the proper equipment and training such a venture would be foolhardy but they'd try it if they had to. They hoped to find a pass of some kind leading through the mountain range.

Again they divided into smaller groups for faster exploration. They knew it might take weeks but even so as the days passed discouragement grew. Gary's group working toward the sea met with forbidding semi-desert land and sheer granite-like cliffs. As discouraging as it appeared they explored laboriously as far as their water and other supplies allowed before turning back. It soon became apparent that it might take years to break out of the imprisonment of their vast valley.

Stacy's group came back to report that after skirting the foothills for several weeks they had come to another row of poison trees with what appeared to be a great, stinking swamp beyond. It was probably the easternmost part of the endless marshy plain that stretched before them across the river at Outer California.

"As scary as those trees were we felt safer on this side of them than being any nearer to that gucky mess," Jeremy commented with a shiver.

It was finally decided to concentrate their efforts on exploring an arm of the forest that seemed to stretch on up through the foothills into the mountains. Hopefully it might lead into a canyon or a pass to the other side. The weary pioneers had strong doubts about this because every turn so far had been blocked in some way but they had to try.

Except for the disappointment of not reaching their goal the exploration was exciting. Martha had always been frustrated by the lack of time to stop and explore every interesting side road, historical monument or forest path, when traveling on Earth. Being the first of their kind to touch this place added spice to every new thing they found. They had become famous trailblazers.

Interest in the missing children had not faded. The telepathic communications were monitored by parents taking turns. Every new adventure, mishap or finding was newsworthy and was released through the legal foundation set up soon after the tragedy. Governmental space agencies were especially interested in any scrap of information. Just as it occurred to the children that a natural phenomenon was not likely to have been the cause of their space journey it also seemed plain to Earth scientists. They were very concerned over what lay behind all of this. It was puzzling to everyone why no contact of any kind with aliens had been made. Had the Earth children been dropped on an uninhabited planet by another civilization as an experiment to prove it habitable? Or, had they been isolated on a portion of an inhabited planet to be watched from afar to study the human race?

# What? Where?

**\*\*\*\***

The campsite was moved closer to the new focal point. Searching here in the forest would be slower. The undergrowth was much heavier and more tangled, seeming to curl and clutch the very base of the mountainside in most spots. The trees were so tall that sunlight was dim even at midday. Though the vegetation was lush there seemed to be very little animal life about. It was so quiet that everyone spoke in subdued voices. Even laughter seemed out of place.

At first they seemed to be making progress. Dave's small group had been able to climb into a small ravine that looked promising but after quite a struggle they came to a dead end. Each time they came to a point where they could go no further, even though they searched painstakingly along the edges of that impenetrable mountain wall in all directions. Sometimes hopes were raised when it was possible to find a place to climb upward but always these precarious handholds led to more difficult spots.

Discouragement grew as well as hunger. Hunting had proved fruitless and none of the plentiful vegetation was edible. Their supplies were growing short. To make matters worse they seemed to have reached the end of the forest, at its highest elevation. As long as the trees had kept on there was hope that it would lead to a pass through the mountains.

They were now camped in a slight clearing where the sheer rock formations lay in slanted folds on both sides of a shallow canyon. The forest lay behind them. Even though this was a dead end there was a small spring of sparkling, clear water which made this a more favorable campsite. It was also warmer with the sun reflecting heat from the rock face.

It was a glum bunch of weary rock climbers who sat in the early evening twilight trying to decide what to do next. Divide the group and send one part back for more supplies while the rest retraced their search patterns or all go back for a rest and time to think of a new approach? There was still the ocean. If they could ever build a seaworthy boat they might try sailing along the coast.

"Look," Tom whispered. "Fresh meat!" All eyes followed his pointing finger. There stood a deer-like creature watching them curiously just beyond the light from the campfire. Dave reached for his bow and set the arrow.

"Dave, wait!" Martha shouted. A chorus of angry, frustrated voices protested that her shout had scared away a very good meal.

"But didn't you see what I saw? We couldn't kill that animal even if we are hungry."

"See what? Chrissy asked.

"That creature is a pet of some kind. It was wearing a collar!"

The delicate brown animal had simply vanished. They might have imagined seeing it except that it's tracks were found near the spring. Where had it gone? Where had it come from?

Now at least, they had proof that they were not the only people on the planet. They were fairly certain the animal had not come from the forest behind them nor fled past them into it but search as they might through the tangled brush at the base of the cliff they could not find the elusive little pet. It had melted into the mountain.

They looked for several hours the next morning but at last weary and hungry they decided to break camp and return to Outer California. While the children rested Martha went to the spring to fill her waterskin. It was rather pleasant in the sunny patch near the water splashing over the rock, so she sat for a while musing about the little creature she'd caught only a glimpse of briefly. Such a gentle looking animal; young too. It would have been nice to be able to pet it and have a look at its collar for clues. Perhaps it could have led them to the way out of the valley.

Something soft nudged her cheek and she reached up to give Rascal an absent-minded scratching. Rascal! His fur didn't feel like that! Turning carefully she saw she was stroking the head of the little animal she'd startled the night before. It wore a carefully braided color of green, white and blue shiny fabric strips fastened with a silver color clasp.

"How did you know I wanted to see you?" she crooned as she stroked its soft fur. Could this animal be summoned by a mental call? Standing, she pictured it following her, sending a soothing thought of safety and it pranced gracefully along beside her wagging its deer-like tail, into camp.

Before Martha rounded the rock into view she called softly ahead warning the children not to rush over and startle their new friend. It seemed happy to meet them all gamboling from one to the other. Even Rascal seemed to like the wee stranger.

"If that 'deerling' can come and go there must be a way out. Maybe it's near here," reasoned the ever practical Barry.

It could be just as lost as we are too, you know," Troy remarked.

"I think it is a young female. We'll try to follow her when she leaves camp," said Martha. "In fact she may be able to communicate telepathically like Bluebelle. I was wishing to see her when she turned up beside me."

"Hey! Wait! I want to see your collar," begged Chrissy as her new friend tried to tug away.

"Let her go. See where she goes."

Following the deerling was simple as she waited or came back if they lost sight of her. She led them straight into the brush and along the rock face. Then almost before their eyes she vanished!

Martha got down on her hands and knees to peer under a large bush and had her nose licked by the deerling peering out of a long, low, cave-like crevice. A cave! This was the only opening to a cave they'd seen since their search started. They had missed it because it was below a shelf of rock behind the bushes. It had never occurred to them to get on their hands and knees and crawl along the rock face. They had been looking for canyons or ravines that might pass through the mountains or a large cave perhaps. Would this small earth fault be a safe passage? How would they explore in the dark?

Hilary was sent for the longest rope they had. The end of it was tied to the trunk of the nearest bush. Martha tied the other end to her waist and squirming flat on her stomach was just able to crawl into the opening. A little of the light from the outside revealed a cave large enough to stand up in though it might be necessary for several of her rapidly growing boys to stoop a little.

The deerling seemed impatient for her to follow so she carefully inched her way forward into the dark. Though Martha had ordered her charges to stay behind until she saw it was safe the suspense was too great. One by one they scrabbled through the opening and followed the rope. It was eerie and disturbing. In total darkness one quickly becomes disoriented. The rope became the only real thing to hang onto. The deerling sensing her distress and impatient to get on, came back and nudged her hand so Martha clung to her collar. Apparently the animal could see in the dark. Just as she thought she saw a very dim light ahead Martha came to the end of the rope.

"Untie it and give it to me," Ron whispered at her elbow. "I'll hold it and the rest can form a chain by hanging on to me. Maybe you can go a bit farther that way."

Following Ron's suggestion gave Martha many more yards of

safety line to reach toward that dim spot ahead. She was just able to reach a large boulder before she had to let go of the impatiently tugging animal who immediately bounded forward up a slight rise making welcoming noises. Martha caught a glimpse of a mass of red curls for an instant as the deerling slipped through a small, sunny opening.

"So that's where you've been hiding," came the thought to Martha. She was sure she hadn't heard anything. "Let me get my permalamp and I'll have a look. Naughty Shanti! I've had to leave my monitor to look for you but I guess it's all right because the subjects are napping and leader is dozing by the spring."

A sudden beam of light stabbing into the darkness caused Martha to duck down behind the sheltering boulder.

"Shanti be careful!" Don't shove! Oh, you made me drop my light. Naughty girl! Now I'll have to climb down your dusty hiding hole to get it. Bother! I can't do it now. I'm due to make my report. Come on you bumbling baby I'm not letting you out of my sight this time."

Quickly Martha crept forward and grabbed the light, retracing her steps to Ron and the end of the rope. They anchored the rope with several rocks and hurried to the cave opening. As they went she briefed them on her impressions. Ron and Kristi had 'heard' the whole mind conversation too. Their curiosity had over-ridden the fear of the complete darkness that had inhibited the transmission to the others.

"We have to get back before she gets to her monitor. Our every move appears to be watched. I wonder if they pick up conversations too?"

Reaching the entrance they scrambled through and then pretended to be playing hide and seek in and out of the bushes before getting back to camp.

Before she crawled out of the cave Martha found the switch

on the permalamp and turned it off. She hid it in her clothing and later sneaked it into her back pack.

Apparently Shanti's owner was already searching for her and away from her monitor when she appeared beside Martha. They had been lucky this time or had they? There had to be other monitors. Were they watched at night? Whatever they did had to be done soon. If they were able to receive impressions could the others receive them? Even now her thoughts might be monitored. It was a scary notion. "Well, Martha decided, "I shouldn't take time to worry about those unknowns."

"Come on and play a new game," she shouted. They all got in a circle on their stomachs, heads almost touching and with a precious piece of chalk, a damp rag and the back of Ron's navy blue nylon jacked they made plans by writing instead of speaking.

They broke camp making things appear ready for an early start the next morning. "End of search, return soon" was sent to the team at Outer California. "All's well," came the reply. It was a shame not to share the secret but they were afraid to give it away. If the aliens found out about their discovery they might block the entrance before they had a chance to use it. Their diary entry was brought up to date with full details and left in Stacy's pack. If they didn't get back the support team might find it when they came searching; though that would take weeks.

Then they settled down to rest until just before dawn trying to keep their minds blank so their thoughts wouldn't give away the plan. They took turns on lookout duty through the night and when Russ's watch, which still worked, showed four a.m. each person quickly roused. Stacy's pack was hopefully hidden from view behind a tree facing away from the mountain. The rest of the gear was taken into the cave.

Using the permalamp it was easy to retrace their steps through the cave. The light was amazing! The intensity and width of the beam could be adjusted so they were able to study some of the cave as they went along. The passage near the entrance seemed to run along a natural fault in the rock with the roof slanting down to a gravel floor. They could walk quite comfortably upright next to the wall on their right. This long crack opened out into a rather large cave beyond the large boulder Martha had reached the previous day, but it appeared to be below ground level because the only outside opening was in the rock face above their heads. Shanti had reached it by climbing up some loose rocks that were piled almost to the opening. It was necessary for them to move other larger rocks to build up the pile before the opening could be climbed to safely. By the time this was done it was already quite light.

# *Look Behind You!*

**\*\*\*\***

O.K., O.K. Shanti. I'll wake up! I see my subjects have gotten an earlier start than I did. After breakfast I'll set the monitor to pick up their trail."

By now the entire group straining for any sound or hint of telepathic communication sensed that exchange with the deerling. Cautiously they all managed to squeeze through the opening and slip into the bushes covering the slopes of the foothills. They were at the end of a long canyon deep into the mountain such as they had hoped to find on the other side. This one widened out gradually from their vantage point until it reached the valley floor. The sight before them was breathtakingly beautiful. Obviously it was an inhabited planet as the distant patchwork of cultivated fields indicated. There seemed to be dwellings but so well designed that they almost blended into the landscape. It was hard to see at this distance but nothing appeared to be moving except the birds at this early morning hour.

We'll have to show ourselves sometime and I'd prefer to meet the natives one at a time, at least at first," Martha said. "Let's approach Shanti's owner cautiously."

Taking great care they crept softly in the direction of a low voice speaking in a strange language. Oddly though they couldn't understand the words they were all able to comprehend some of the meaning, probably the mental intent.

A slender figure dressed in a light blue uniform was nodding a head of large red curls at a double-screened portable console as she twisted dials and spoke to someone. Apparently she was searching for her subjects for the pioneers could see that one of the screens was scanning their camp and on to their trail. While this was going on she was talking to a face visible on the other screen.

"They must have left camp before sun-up as they aren't there. I'm scanning their trail now. Don't worry I'll find them."

"I'm sure you will! Look behind you Kayla."

Slowly the figure at the console turned to face the group of teenagers standing with their teacher and smiling in her direction.

Shanti bounded forward happily and Martha dropped to her knees to greet the friendly animal. Rascal edged out of the crowd to renew his acquaintance.

The frightened girl did not appear to be very different from themselves. She was quite slender with deep-set red-brown eyes without lashes or brows, nostrils but very little nose, thin lips and lots of freckles. It wasn't until later that they noticed she had only four fingers on each hand and no outer ears.

"Don't be afraid, we want to be friends," said Martha.

"How did you get through the mountains," gasped Kayla.

"We followed Shanti. You speak English well. Where did you learn it?"

"I had to learn it from the tape scanner if I wanted to be part of the project. Now I really am in trouble. I was sent to this remote station because I gave you a warning about the wave and now they'll think I let you out."

"Were we to be kept isolated forever?' Barry asked.

"No, but I don't know when you were to be contacted, that's up to the senior scientists. Hey he looks almost like me!" Kayla pointed at Mark. "Only his hair is straighter."

"Why were we kept alone in the first place?" Chrissy wanted to know.

Kayla told them briefly what she knew about the project whose basic aim was to study Earth people before making contact with the planet itself. "You are a comparatively young civilization and we have been watching you from afar for over fifty years. I haven't even read all of the background data, there is so much of it. In recent times the turmoil on your world and the weapons you are developing are alarming to us. We are not sure we want to make contact because we might find it was wrong to do so. There are so many different types of people too. You see we are all very similar. We have to be cautious about definite contact because we might be destroyed by your aggressiveness. Earthmen often seem to shoot first and ask questions later. We tried to make radio contact but it was always treated as a joke or those who did believe us were thought to have mental problems. So we brought you here to see how you would survive and find out if you were worthwhile beings."

"I do hope that we won't be forced to remain in isolation. We are anxious to learn more about our new world. Nor do we want to be separated from the team waiting for us at Outer California. Perhaps we had better send some volunteers back to tell them what has happened. That way if we do get cut off we'll have someone on both sides of the mountain who knows we finally made contact."

"That won't be necessary." Martha was interrupted by the arrival of several red-bearded men wearing the same blue uniforms. Their leader went on to tell them that the entrance to the cave would not be sealed but until they were tested for possible harmful virus' and immunity to the known diseases of Sularis they wouldn't be allowed to mingle with the natives. Except for Kayla, she had already been exposed.

"Sir," Ron asked politely, "Have you been aiding our transmissions to Earth in some way?"

Terrell, the senior science leader of the group smiled. "Yes we have. We wanted your parents to know you were still alive. We knew that because of their grief they would more likely believe all this was possible making future contact easier. Young man no questions now, they'll be answered later." This to the irrepressible Barry who was about to ask a stream of questions about the manner of their transportation, the incredible speed of their travel and where were they? Ron was as eager to know how thought transmission could be boosted as Barry was to get answers to his questions but he was able to mask his curiosity with polite calm.

When the government had sealed off the great peninsula to make a primitive preserve for the kidnapped children the cave opening had not been there. A later rock fall had revealed it to the ever curious Shanti. The poison trees had been planted to keep the children from finding the way down to the beach at that point. It was carefully concealed but they might have found it except for the failing light as the end of the day. The boulders had been placed to keep them off the ramp way too, as there was no way of warning them about the annual tidal wave without revealing the presence of another civilization. Poison trees were also planted to keep them out of the dangerous marsh at the easternmost part of the valley. If Stacy's group had gotten through and kept close to the foot of the mountains they would have eventually come to the great pass with a highway to the interior. However her party would not have gotten past that point. The huge gates closing off the roads to the beach during the flood time were closed and had been while the area was being used for the science preserve much to the displeasure of the people who loved to frequent the beach.

"We hadn't counted on your persistence in searching, especially in the young. Just another of the signs of your intelligent approach to survival we have been pleased to note. Though we didn't think you'd be so successful at getting out before we wanted you to," Terrell commented.

"Kayla will go back with you through the cave tunnel. We'll enlarge the opening a little so we can explore that cave more later. Supplies and a portable communisol unit will be dropped on the other side. By the time you've reached your "Outer California" our space council will have met and decided where we go from here. Do inform your parents in your messages that you've made contact with us and to be prepared for more direct communication."

The trip back through the cave seemed to go more quickly this time. There was no need for stealth and several permalamps chased away the darkness. It was fortunate that they had left the rope guide in place as the cave proved to be much larger than they had suspected and with many side passages.

"Hope we have time to come back and explore this someday," said Jon wistfully.

By the time they had reached the other side Kayla's supplies and com unit had been dropped.

"Don't you have transportation so we won't have to hike all the way back?" complained Troy

Of course we do but this is a wilderness preserve and only emergency vehicles are allowed. We try to live with the nature not dominate or destroy it. Besides Terrell needs the time to report to his committee and meet with the Space Council," Kayla explained.

"Its a shame we can't make more detailed contact with our home team and tell them what's happened. They're already feeling a bit left out I imagine," Martha commented. "If you can assist thought transmission you must have very advanced communications systems."

"If you had some sort of receiver on the other end we could."

"The old public address loudspeaker is still on the wall of the classroom above the chalk board maybe they could beam into that somehow."

"I'll ask Terrell right now. I have to test the com unit anyway," Kayla promised.

While Kayla tested her equipment the others fixed lunch using some of the new supplies to supplement their own diminished stores.

"I think I can get through but only one way. Central Com gave me directions for setting my signals and they will boost it through.

Everyone gathered around the small twin-screened com unit as Kayla adjusted the dials and switches. Soon the inside of the classroom appeared on the transparent square on front of them.

"How can they do that without a camera?" Barry questioned.

"We've perfected a long distance photo probe that operates in a more sophisticated manner than I can explain," replied Kayla.

"There's no one there!"

"Look Raquel has a new batch of kittens."

"There's Beth. Look Bluebelle is pulling her!" Indeed Bluebelle had gripped a bit of Beth's skirt and was urgently tugging her along. Somehow the space chicken had sensed the need for someone to be in the room and had grabbed the person nearest to the building to urge inside.

"Beth," Martha spoke softly. Beth looked around startled. "Don't be afraid. We've made contact with the people of this planet and they're helping us to talk to you through the wall speaker. Go get the others please."

Quickly the girl left the room and returned with Tina, Amy and Vickie who were obviously very excited.

"I can speak to you and see you if you are in front of the speaker but you can't answer back. Get one of the small practice chalkboards and write in large letters so we'll be able to see your messages. Where are the boys?"

"Melon-picking," Amy wrote rapidly.

Quickly Martha told them briefly what had happened; that they were on their way back; and to send "Made contact-peaceful, intelligent people", in their nightly message to Earth.

After quickly eating a pleasant lunch, the group lost no time in getting on the trail for Outer California. Kayla carried her comunit which was amazingly light for such a complicated piece of equipment. The rest of her supplies were divided out and carried by the others. Kayla was very interested in all that she saw as this was all new territory for her. The hiking went very quickly over the now familiar ground as the children pointed out or explained things to their new traveling companion.

# *Earth-Shaking News!*

### \*\*\*\*

Outer California's electrifying message of contact with other intelligent beings startled a worried, weary population. Economic slumps, armed squabbles between smaller nations, illegal political conniving and a worsening ecology served to keep many people in a near state of hopeless depression. The word peaceful in the message from outer space was indeed a good sign but with so little to go on no other conclusions could be drawn. In fact there were many, mostly emerging nations and the more uneducated peoples who found it hard to believe in any of it at all, including moon landings and space flights. The major nations of Earth now had a much larger problem to concentrate on than just their planet's concerns. It was clear that most of the world's problems would have to be settled before a united front could handle whatever came from deep space. Until they had more proof nothing could be decided about the space contacts but at least the problems at home suddenly appeared to be of secondary importance.

The parents of the children were even more hopeful. Especially when a later message read "Direct contact soon". Belief in psychic contact was all they had had up to now and sometimes hope was the only thing that supported that belief. News media interest had faded a little of late. This new development was viewed by a few as a fake attempt to renew this interest, so that the fees they paid for the press releases would continue to go into the trust funds established for the absent children and their teacher.

"Interrupt newscast- ready to record." That message almost set off a riot among the parents present. As many of them who could manage to, were attending the evening sessions now and the room was crowded.

"Mom, you're still smoking!" The silent rebuke from Beth

startled the whole room into murmurs of astonishment. It was the first time they'd had any proof that the children had received any visual impressions from Earth.

Indeed it was the first time any of the children had seen anything from Earth since they'd left it. The scientists of Sularis had placed a communications space station so they could interrupt and use one of Earth's satellites. With this as a relay station the telepathy messages could also be boosted and visual impressions sent both ways. This was not needed for long however.

Shortly after the search parties rejoined the Outer California team, a group of Sularian scientists arrived on a silent aircar which they deftly set down in the clearing near the classroom, neatly missing the cookfire pit.

After Kayla introduced her new friends to the scientists, events progressed swiftly. All were given physical exams by the doctors and pronounced in the best of health. Even Amy's leg had mended properly much to Martha's relief.

A zoologist and a veterinarian examined Rascal, Raquel and all the various kittens. Kayla wanted to find homes for the extras if the scientists agreed. There wouldn't be any problems placing the small felines. Being other world specimens they'd be much in demand as pets.

Agriculture specialists were given a tour of the gardens where they avidly took samples of the Earth vegetables and later the apple and orange trees.

Terrell arrived in a second car with a party of officials and social scientists eager to study the children and their surroundings first hand. Arrangements had been made for the first visual-vocal contact with Earth. A communication space station would relay transmissions through an Earth satellite.

Even though permission to leave their primitive area had been granted, the Americans, as they asked to be called, decided that the first broadcast should come from Outer California. The Sularians had to agree that seeing the familiar building in unfamiliar surroundings would be more convincing than seeing the children in a completely new setting.

Shortly after six one evening, telecasts world-wide were interrupted. In the United States the latest pet-food commercial preceding the evening news winked out to be replaced by an unfamiliar but polite voice apologizing for the interruption and urging a standby for a spacecast.

Just as suddenly as the interruption of the regular program had begun, the spacecast started. A view of the kidnapped classroom and it's human inhabitants appeared on TV screens all over the world. Before anyone could speak a grinning teenager jumped up, waved and said, "Hi gang", causing a ripple of embarrassed laughter from his classmates.

As eager as they were to talk to their families almost all of the group was seized with stage fright. Not Tom. His airy "Hi gang", loosened them all up as he popped up in front of Mrs. Stern and Terrell, when the formal broadcast began.

"Thank you Tom," said Martha trying to suppress a grin as she introduced Terrell and the head of the Sularian Space Council, who in turn presented the Sularian president. After his brief formal message of peace and good will the president stepped aside to allow more personal messages from each of the young people to their families. When that part of the broadcast was over a technical team completed the transmission with explanations for the setting up of further communications.

The temporary classroom building used as an office by the parent monitors almost rocked off its supports with the joyous commotion within as the spacecast ended. Instant snapshots taken during the program were studied closely and tapes replayed. Comments were exchanged over how well the children looked, how they'd grown and remarks made about several of the boys whose voices had changed. Even those with the greatest doubts were convinced and reassured.

Leading newscasters, recovering quickly, began solemn interpretations of the earth-shaking event. Government meetings were hastily convened foreign countries rushed translations as the spacecast was given in English since those involved were Americans. The world began its adjustment to the proof that it was not the only civilized planet in the universe.

# Beyond the Mountain At Last

**\*\*\*\***

When the spacecast was over the children and their pets were taken by air car to the Capital city of Sularis, Sula. From the air the pleasant city stretched in a well planned arrangement of buildings, parks and moving walkways. None of the buildings appeared to be over ten stories high; many were multi-level with bright rooftop gardens everywhere. The light colored buildings gave the whole city a happy look.

"I don't see any cars or buses," said Lee.

Terrell explained that no one owned a private vehicle. Moving sidewalks and underground subways were used to get from place to place within the city. Even deliveries of furniture, merchandise, and supplies were handled by special freight sections underground, directly to factories, stores and apartment buildings. Even outlying country homes and farms were serviced by non-polluting government vehicles.

"How large is your planet?" asked Ron.

"About four times as large as Earth, roughly the size of the planet you call Uranus. But we haven't explored or colonized all of it yet. Our ancestors came from another galaxy and were sent to colonize Sularis. They were charged by their charter to profit by the mistakes of the home planet and to proceed with caution to enhance not destroy their new environment. Thus we expand slowly using only what we need of our resources as we do so. While we have been doing this we have also been observing Earth to determine if we might accept some colonists and if it would be safe to propose membership in the Space Federation. That would be to your advantage as your planet could benefit much from sharing of our advanced knowledge. We have very grave doubts about your fitness as a planet to join a peaceful organization."

Before Barry could protest about Terrell's last statement the air cars had swooped down to land quickly and gracefully at Sula's main transport terminal. The Americans were not prepared for the vast crown of curious Sularians who awaited their arrival. Just as their parents had followed what little there was to know back on Earth the Sularians had followed the published accounts and the few photos taken from the com unit screens with great interest. They were eager to see the Earthlings in person.

Red-haired Mark seemed to cause the most interest, probably because he looked most like themselves. From Kristi's bright blonde to Stacy's rich brunette every range of hair color was represented, most of it long and straight, a great contrast to the very short curly red of the native population. The differences in eye colors and shapes of noses were commented on widely. The American children felt like they were on parade in a zoo.

Despite feeling like part of a sideshow they were staring just as hard. The girls were relieved to see that the blue uniforms of the space science teams weren't worn by everybody. Some of the clothes worn by the women in the eager crowd were very interesting. Because they all looked so much alike physically it appeared as though the Sularians tried hard for individuality in dress.

Tom waved and smiled. The Sularians who had watched the first broadcast to Earth recognized him immediately and waved back.

In the center of the gleaming, spacious terminal a platform had been built and banked with colorful flowers. After short, formal speeches of welcome by important officials the Americans were introduced one by one and assigned by pairs to host families. The science team had decided that living with a Sularian family would be the quickest way to become acquainted with their planet's mode of life. Martha and Rascal would stay with Terrell and his family.

Kayla was almost as much an attraction as the teenagers for she carried a cage of kittens who protested loudly at the unfamiliar confinement. They would soon be placed in new homes but for the moment they were very unhappy.

During the next few weeks the Americans were kept very busy learning about the peaceful people of Sularis and becoming familiar with the colonized parts of the planet. Each one had also had several opportunities to speak with his or her family on Earth. Ever since the first spacecast technicians on both planets had worked to set up a good communications system. Now the scientists and diplomats were verbally maneuvering, setting up a time and place for the first meetings on Earth between the Sularians and Americans. Even at this stage of affairs there were still those few who believed the whole thing to be a giant hoax.

Dealing with survival had been very difficult at times but Martha Stern soon realized that she almost preferred those problems to those of diplomacy. Because she was the adult member of the captive group it was inevitable that she'd be drawn into the position of Earth representative, if only temporarily.

The Sularians were reluctant to send anyone to Earth to represent them until they were completely sure that their envoys would be safe, not just captive freaks.

Finally a plan was worked out that was satisfactory to both sides. A large Sularian space ship would land at the naval base in Northern California close to the teenager's hometown. From this protected environment diplomatic negotiations would continue. All the Americans would return to Earth aboard the ship but not all would be allowed to leave it at the same time though parents would be allowed to visit freely. As soon as the scientists and diplomats volunteering for duty on Sularis passed psychological and physical testing, they and their families would be exchanged for the students and their teacher. A contingent of Sularians had volunteered to remain behind to set up the Sularian Embassy.

# *Homeward Bound*

**\*\*\*\***

"There they are," shouted Jeff as the last to arrive, Kristi and Beth, stepped from the gleaming subway car that had brought them from their host's home to the central station where they were to meet the others.

"Come on!  Hurry up!" urged Vicki excitedly.

Everyone was so stirred up about the impending trip back to Earth that the air around them seemed charged with excess energy. Kayla and Terrell had been assigned as part of the research team going on the voyage.  They hurried up and joined the eager group of travelers boarding the special train to the launch site.

Safely outside the city limits the transport system emerged from its underground tunnel to become a quiet monorail capable of carrying passengers swiftly to the most distant parts of the colonies. The comfortable, air-conditioned cars traveled within a self-contained force field which protected any wildlife from wandering into its path.  The carefully designed railway was scarcely noticeable so the environment remained as natural as possible.

The spaceport was situated in the caldera of an extinct volcano.  The approach to it was signaled by again going underground and the gradual slowing down of the subway cars. Terrell explained how old lava tubes or fumaroles were used whenever possible as tunnels through the mountain.  Caves had been enlarged and more carved out as needed to house the laboratories, workshops and living quarters.

The travellers were checked in at the main gate and assigned temporary quarters.  At the same time they received their schedules for the briefing meetings they would have to attend.  When all these necessary details had been taken care of they were free to wander about before the evening meal several hours away.

All were eager to see the space ship and Terrell agreed to guide them through the unfamiliar tunnels of the base to the natural bowl in the center of the volcano where the ship was berthed. They had expected the ship to be very large but the Americans were nearly struck speechless by their first sight of the great, elliptical shape nestled on the floor of the caldera, its burnished sides glimmering softly in the sunlight.

"I don't see how you carried us in that without our knowing it," Rick remarked. Voto, a senior engineer, assigned to escort their tour of the base, explained how under cover of the rainstorm the crew of the space ship had created a whirling vortex much like the funnel cloud of a tornado which tore the classroom free and forced it airborne. "Our force field temporarily disrupted your defense surveillance system and your building was drawn to the bottom of the ship undetected. We then covered it with a transparent bubble of a special material capable of resisting the tremendous stresses of space travel. Remember it was so dark you couldn't see outside and you very helpfully had your students duck under their desks," he mentioned to the teacher. "Atmospheric pressures were kept at Earth level and breathing easily, kept balanced within the bubble. After we were sure, by monitoring your conversations, that you had seen Earth receding in space we pumped a mild drug into the atmosphere of your bubble to keep you asleep until we had placed the building where we wanted it on Sularis. You spent more time traveling than you thought."

The inside of the huge ship was almost a miniature city. It took more than a day to explore it and still the group felt that they hadn't seen enough. Quarters were assigned and souvenirs stowed away. Kristi had been allowed to bring Bluebelle though the veterinarian had cautioned her that the space chicken was getting very old and might not live much longer. Most everyone brought their pets except Ron who had left his with his host family because his father was allergic to cats.

Lift-off was scheduled for the next day so after the final briefing meeting where they learned that all but a few persons would be suspended in a sleep state for most of the trip, the Americans went out for a last look around the crater. In a way it was sad to be leaving Sularis. Adventure once tasted, creates an appetite for more. There was more than a little worry about readapting to Earth and their families. After all they had been gone nearly five years living on their own.

The sun had moved past midheaven so shadows were beginning to creep down the steep sides of the caldera. Magnificent shades of blues and purples sliding into the browns and blacks of the volcanic rocks reminded them of the times they had watched the distant mountain ranges from Outer California and how they had speculated about what lay beyond them.

Lee's comment that he wished he didn't have to sleep through all the exciting parts was loudly seconded by many of the others.

"Well I hate to admit it but I'm going to miss the place," said Tom.

"We'll all miss it in one way or another, Tom," reassured Martha. "Come on, we're due in the scientists' mess hall for the farewell dinner."

The festive dinner in the gaily decorated mess hall had lasted until quite late so no one had trouble getting to sleep. Getting up was another matter for a few reluctant sleepyheads. Once awake however, everyone dressed quickly and ate a hasty breakfast. This time they were all determined not to miss the excitement of the liftoff.

The experienced crew went about their tasks with smooth efficiency having done their jobs many times before. The animals were already secure in their special cages so the excited passengers busied themselves with the harnesses on their contoured seats. Each was positioned so there was a good line of sight to a special viewing screen for watching the liftoff by remote camera. Later before going to sleep they would have the chance to look at Sularis as they orbited the planet before heading into deep space for the journey to Earth.

"I wonder when we'll start our takeoff," Margaret asked.

"We already have, look at the screen," Jenny answered.

The takeoff was accomplished so smoothly they were scarcely aware of it. Soon Kayla and Terrell joined them at the viewports just as fascinated to see their planet from space as were the others. It was an awesome sight but before they had the chance to become bored with watching they were directed to their bunks.

"When are we going to sleep?" a drowsy Michele asked the cabin attendant.

"You'd be surprised how long you've been sleeping already," he replied. "If you look out the view port I think you'll see quite a different planet from Sularis."

"Hey everybody look! Earth!" Michele shouted. No one needed a second invitation. There before their eyes was the familiar planet they thought they'd never see again. They orbited Earth while the formal docking arrangements were completed. Within the ship apprehension and excitement grew. The Sularians were now able to understand how the Americans felt at first, as they wondered how they would be accepted by the people of Earth.

With everyone securely belted in the great ship began a careful descent and approach to the naval airfield selected for their landing. It was fascinating to watch the curves of the planet disappear, the lines of North America become clear and then San Francisco Bay was recognized.

"I can bring her in from here," Troy boasted.

"Don't worry the pilot of this thing is doing great," Chrissy countered.

Everyone in the bay area must have been on the freeway it was so jammed. There were people standing everywhere outside watching the sky. As they drew closer to setting down the United States Marine Corp guards, arms locked could be seen holding back the crowds pressing hard to get a closer look at the specially prepared landing area. Dignitaries and families waited in a cordoned off enclosure to greet the space travelers.

Terrell warned the Americans that they might suffer some discomfort with their first breaths of their native atmosphere after living on pollution-free Sularis. He privately hoped he could stand it gracefully. He'd been dismayed at the sludgy appearance of the air as they came down toward the landing.

As soon as the Sularian ship had settled the exit ramp rolled out smoothly from the softly gleaming hull. The teacher led the students of the longest unscheduled field trip in history down the ramp to greet the families who had been allowed to approach the ship. Formal welcomes and frustrated newsmen would have to wait. After greeting her family Martha finally remembered her duties and introduced the Sularian delegation to the commander of the base who took charge of the more formal arrangements.

Because of the careful preparations beforehand everything went well. World leaders were soon meeting with the Sularian officials. The teenagers, by now celebrities, were reunited with families and friends. Mrs. Stern regretfully gave Rascal back to his rightful owners.

The Sularian science team met with the eager Earth scientists to start the screening of persons wanting to go to Sularis and there were thousands of volunteers.

When at last, several weeks later, the first negotiations had been completed satisfactorily and the diplomats, scientists and news media representatives chosen, the Sularian ship rose majestically for the return trip. On the passenger list was a familiar name. After a short visit with his family Mark had asked permission to return to Sularis as Earth's first volunteer colonist.

## *About The Author*

Mary Starner, now a retired teacher, grew up in Connecticut. When she and her husband grew tired of muggy summers, mosquitos and endless sludgy winters they moved to Palo Alto, California to raise their three daughters. She accepted a position in the Los Altos, California schools. At that time, as part of the fourth grade language arts curriculum students were required to write a paragraph a day to share with the class. One day after something suddenly startled them all Mrs. Starner suggested they each write an explanation of what had happened saying she would do that too. The class liked her version so much they wanted more. This led to the book. After several rejections from publishers she set the manuscript aside, but even after all these years, someone from that group will ask if it was ever published. Here it is at last, dedicated to Room 18, Hillview School's class of 1972-73.

.

Made in the USA
San Bernardino, CA
04 February 2017